Hauk lay awake. Wide awake.

As a rule, he possessed considerable discipline when it came to the time for sleep. He'd been trained well. Sleep was a main building block of superior performance. As he'd told Elli—

He caught his own dangerous thoughts up short. Not simply Elli. Never simply Elli.

She was the princess. Her Highness. *Princess* Elli.

He couldn't allow his thoughts to become too familiar. It was forbidden. This was the daughter of the king. And something was happening to him, in this period of forced proximity with her. Something that had never happened to him before.

He let himself think it. *I want her....*

D1054777

Dear Reader,

Not only does Special Edition bring you the joys of life, love and family—but we also capitalize on our authors' many talents in storytelling. In our spotlight, Christine Rimmer's exciting new miniseries, VIKING BRIDES, is the epitome of innovative reading. The first book, *The Reluctant Princess,* details the transformation of an everyday woman to glorious royal—with a Viking lover to match! Christine tells us, "For several years, I've dreamed of creating a modern-day country where the ways of the legendary Norsemen would still hold sway. I imagined what fun it would be to match up the most macho of men, the Vikings, with contemporary American heroines. Oh, the culture clash—oh, the lovely potential for lots of romantic fireworks! This dream became VIKING BRIDES." Don't miss this fabulous series!

Our Readers' Ring selection is Judy Duarte's *Almost Perfect,* a darling tale of how good friends fall in love as they join forces to raise two orphaned kids. This one will get you talking! Next, Gina Wilkins delights us with *Faith, Hope and Family,* in which a tormented heroine returns to save her family and faces the man she's always loved. You'll love Elizabeth Harbison's *Midnight Cravings,* in which a sassy publicist and a small-town police chief fall hard for each other and give in to a sizzling attraction.

The Unexpected Wedding Guest, by Patricia McLinn, brings together an unlikely couple who share an unexpected kiss. Newcomer to Special Edition Kate Welsh is no stranger to fresh plot twists, in *Substitute Daddy,* in which a heroine carries her deceased twin's baby and has feelings for the last man on earth she should love—her snooty brother-in-law.

As you can see, we have a story for every reader's taste. Stay tuned next month for six more top picks from Special Edition!

Sincerely,

Karen Taylor Richman
Senior Editor

Please address questions and book requests to:
Silhouette Reader Service
U.S.: 3010 Walden Ave., P.O. Box 1325, Buffalo, NY 14269
Canadian: P.O. Box 609, Fort Erie, Ont. L2A 5X3

Christine Rimmer

THE RELUCTANT PRINCESS

SPECIAL EDITION™

Published by Silhouette Books

America's Publisher of Contemporary Romance

This one's for you, Susan Mallery, because you are not
only a fabulous writer and most terrific friend, you can
also plot circles around the best of 'em and you know
when to give encouragement and when to come out
with the gentle reminder that passion is everything.

SILHOUETTE BOOKS

ISBN 0-373-24537-8

THE RELUCTANT PRINCESS

Copyright © 2003 by Christine Rimmer

Printed in U.S.A.

CHRISTINE RIMMER

came to her profession the long way around. Before settling down to write about the magic of romance, she'd been an actress, a salesclerk, a janitor, a model, a phone sales representative, a teacher, a waitress, a playwright and an office manager. She insists she never had a problem keeping a job—she was merely gaining "life experience" for her future as a novelist. Christine is grateful not only for the joy she finds in writing, but for what waits when the day's work is through: a man she loves, who loves her right back, and the privilege of watching their children grow and change day to day. She lives with her family in Oklahoma.

THE RELUCTANT PRINCESS

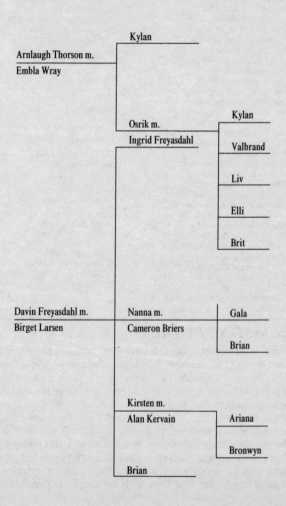

Chapter One

A Viking was the last thing Elli Thorson expected to find in her living room on that sunny afternoon in early May.

At a few minutes after five that day, Elli parked her little silver BMW in her space behind her building and got her two bags of groceries out of the trunk. She'd had the checker bag her purchases in paper because she was short on paper bags. Possibly, if she'd gone ahead and taken plastic, everything would have turned out differently.

With plastic, she would have been carrying the bags low, by the handles. There'd have been nothing in the way of her vision. She'd have seen the Viking before she shut the door to the landing with both of them on the same side of it. Maybe, with the door standing open, there would have been at least a *chance* of escaping him.

When she got up the stairs to her apartment, she was carrying the bags high in her arms, with her purse looped over her left elbow and her key ready in her right hand. Maybe if she hadn't been ready with the key—if she'd set the bags down, dug around in her purse, and opened the door before picking the bags up again...

But she didn't set the bags down. She had her key ready. And on such small choices, the course of a life can depend.

Elli braced the right-hand bag against the door. That freed her hand just enough to work the top lock. Then, by bending her knees and twisting sideways a fraction, she was able to slip the key into the bottom lock and get it open, too. She pushed the door inward, juggling the bags back to where she had a firm grip on them from underneath.

Her apartment had a small entry area—a square of floor, really—between the living room and the kitchen. Elli spun over the threshold. A quick nudge of her heel as she turned to the right and the door swung shut and latched. Her cute little butcher-block kitchen table was right there. She slid the bags onto it.

"Ta-da!" With a flourish, she dropped her keys and purse beside the bags and spun back toward the living area.

That was when she saw him.

He stood in her living room. A man dressed all in black—black slacks, black boots, muscle-hugging black T-shirt. He was blond and scarred and stone-faced—and big. Very, very big.

Elli was no midget herself. She stood five-eleven in bare feet. But this man topped her by several inches. And all of him was broad and hard and thick with muscle. The sheer size of him was scary, even if he hadn't been standing right there in the middle of her living room, uninvited, unexpected and unwelcome in the extreme.

The sight of him so shocked her that she jumped back and let out a shriek.

The man, gazing so calmly at her through piercing gray-blue eyes, fisted a hand and laid it on his chest, right over his heart. "Princess Elli, I bring greetings from your father, King Osrik of Gullandria." His voice was deep and sonorous, his tone grave.

It was then, when he called her Princess Elli, that she realized he was, in reality, a Viking and not some buff burglar she'd just caught in the act. He was a Viking because that was what they were, essentially—the people of Gullandria.

Gullandria. Though Elli had been born there, the place had always seemed to her like something from a fairy tale, a barely remembered bedtime story told to her by her mother.

But Gullandria was real enough. It was an island shaped roughly like a heart that could be found between the Shetlands and Norway, in the Norwegian Sea—a tiny pocket of the world where the ways of the legendary Norsemen still held sway.

Elli's mother, Ingrid Freyasdahl, had been eighteen when she married Osrik Thorson, who shortly thereafter became king of that land. Five years later, Ingrid left the king forever, taking her tiny triplet daughters and returning to California where she'd been born and raised. It had been a big scandal at the time—and now and then the old story still cropped up in tabloid magazines. In those magazines, her mother was always referred to as the Runaway Gullandrian Queen.

Elli's heart was beating way too fast. So what if her father had sent this man? She had no memory of her father. She knew only what her mother had told her and what she'd read in those occasional absurd scandal-sheet exposés. Osrik Thorson seemed no more real to her than the mythical-sounding country where he ruled.

She demanded, "How did you get in here?"

The intruder opened his fist and extended his massive hand, palm out, in a salute. Tattooed in the heart of that hand was a gold-and-blue lightning bolt. "Hauk FitzWyborn, the king's warrior, bloodsworn to your father, His Majesty, King Osrik of the House of Thor. I am at your service, Princess."

She resisted the urge to shrink back from that giant hand and boldly taunted, "Was that my question? I don't think that was my question."

The huge man looked somewhat pained. "It seemed wiser, Your Highness, to be waiting for you inside."

"Wiser than knocking on my door like any normal, civilized human being?"

In answer to that, she got a fractional nod of his big blond head.

"Here in America, what you did is called breaking and entering. What's wise about that?"

This time the fractional move was a shrug.

Elli's mind raced. She felt threatened, boxed in—and at the same time determined that this oversize interloper would not see her fear.

She looked at him sideways. "You said you were at my service."

"I am bloodsworn to your father. That means I serve you, as well."

"Great. To serve me best, you can get out of my apartment."

He had those bulging, tendon-ridged arms crossed over that enormous chest and he didn't look as if he was going anywhere. He said, "Your father wishes your presence at court. He wishes to see you, to speak with you. He has...important matters to discuss with you."

This was all so insulting. Elli felt her cheeks burning. "My father has made zero effort over the years to get in touch with me. What is so important that I have to drop everything and rush to see him now?"

"Allow me to take you to him. His Majesty will explain all."

"Listen. Listen very carefully." Elli employed the same patient, firm tone she often used on stubborn five-year-olds in her class of kindergartners. "I want you to return to Gullandria. When you get there, you can tell my father that if he suddenly just *has* to speak with me, he can pick up the phone and call me. Once he's told me what's going on, *I'll* decide whether I'm willing to go see him or not."

The Viking's frown deepened. Evidently, he found the disparity between her wishes and his orders vaguely troubling. But not troubling enough to get him to give up and go. "You will pack now, Princess," he intoned. "Necessities only. All your needs will be provided for at Isenhalla."

Isenhalla. Ice hall. The silver-slate palace of Gullandrian kings....

Truly, truly weird. A Viking in her living room. A Viking who thought he was taking her to her father's palace. "I guess you haven't been listening. I said, I am going nowhere with you and you are trespassing. I want you to leave."

"You will pack now, please." Those flinty eyes seemed to see right through her and that amazingly square jaw looked set in granite.

Elli repeated, more strongly than the first time, "I said, I want you to leave."

"And once you are packed, I will do as you say. We will leave together."

There was a silence—a loaded one. She glared at him and he stared, unblinking, back at her. From outside, she heard ordinary, everyday sounds: birds singing, the honk of a horn, a leaf blower starting up, a siren somewhere far off in the distance.

Those sounds had the strangest effect on her. They made her want to burst into tears. Though they were right outside her door, those sounds, all at once, seemed lost to her.

Lost...

The word made her think of the brothers she had never known. There had been two of them, Kylan and

Valbrand. Kylan had died as a young child. But Valbrand had grown up in Gullandria with their father, the king. Over the years, she and her sisters had talked about what it might be like to meet their surviving brother someday, to get to know him.

But that would never happen now.

Valbrand was dead, too. Like Kylan.

And were her brothers the key to what was happening here? Her father had no sons anymore. And without a son, maybe his thrown-away daughters had value to him now—whether they wanted anything to do with him, or not.

Yes. She supposed that made sense—or it *would* make sense if she could even be certain that this Viking had been sent by her father in the first place.

Maybe this was a trick. Maybe this man had been sent by an *enemy* of her father's. Or maybe he was simply a criminal, as she'd assumed at first. But instead of robbing her apartment, he was here to take her hostage. He'd haul her out of here and hold her prisoner and her mother would be getting a ransom note....

Oh, she didn't know. How could she know? This was all so confusing.

And whatever the reasons for the Viking in her living room, there could be no more denials. Elli could see it, shining there, in those unwavering pale eyes. Hauk FitzWyborn—who called himself the king's warrior, who said he was blood-something-or-other to her father—*might* be at her service, but only if her desires didn't conflict with whatever orders he'd been given. He intended to take her...somewhere.

And wherever that somewhere actually was, he meant to take her today—whether she agreed to go or not.

The bottom line: this was a kidnapping and Elli was the kidnappee.

Oh, what was she *thinking*—to have stood here and argued with him? She should have hit the door running at the sight of him.

Maybe she could still escape—if she moved fast enough.

She spun for the door.

And she made it. She had the doorknob in her hand.

But she never got a chance to turn it.

With stunning speed for such a big man, he was upon her, wrapping those bulging, scarred arms around her. It was like being engulfed by a warm boulder. She cried out—once. And then a massive hand covered her mouth and nose.

That hand held a soft cloth, a cloth that smelled sharp and bitter.

Drugged. He had *drugged* her....

"Forgive me, Your Highness," she heard him whisper.

And the world went black.

Chapter Two

Hauk looked down at the princess in his arms.

She was slim, but not small, with long, graceful bones and surprisingly large, ripe-looking breasts, the kind of breasts that would serve equally to please a man and nourish the children he gave her. Her mouth was full-lipped—and silent, at the moment. Silent and lax.

The compliant one, his lord had called her. And compliant she was—now. The drug had made her so. But Hauk had looked deep into those fjord-blue eyes. He'd seen the steel at the core. If his lord hoped this one might be yielding when conscious, he was in for an unpleasant surprise.

"Bring her to me," Hauk's lord had instructed. *"Tell her that her father would like to see her, to speak with her. Say that her father has many things*

to say to her and will explain all as soon as he can talk to her. Try to coax her to come with you willingly. My spies tell me that of the three, she is by far the most compliant.''

Hauk had sworn to do as his lord commanded. *"And if she should refuse, in the end, to accompany me?''*

There had been a silence. A silence that spoke volumes. Finally his lord had said quietly, *"Her refusal is not an option. I wish you to bring her. But please. Treat her gently.''*

Shaking his head, Hauk carried the woman to the couch against the inner wall. Coaxing was for courtiers, he thought as he carefully laid her down. He tucked a bright-colored pillow beneath her head so her neck would not be strained into an uncomfortable position. Then he slipped off her low-heeled shoes and smoothed her skirt modestly over those pretty knees.

He stood back and stared down at her, considering. The drug would wear off shortly. She would not be pleased when she woke, and she would make her displeasure known. He should disable her now.

But he hated to do it. She looked so sweet and peaceful, lying there.

With some regret, he went for the duffel bag he'd left behind the chair across the room. From it, he took lengths of soft, strong rope and a kerchief-sized gag.

Carefully, he turned the princess on her side, so she was facing the wall.

He was good with knots. It took only a few minutes to bind her wrists behind her, to tie her knees together, and her slim ankles, as well. He ran an extra length of rope down her back, connecting the ropes at wrist and ankle, bending her knees slightly, drawing her feet up and back.

Perhaps the final rope, which would gradually pull tighter with resistance, was overkill. But he couldn't afford to take any chances. She would be angry when she woke and ready for a fight, ready to do anything in her power to escape. It was his job to see that she *had* no power. He tied the gag firmly in place, taking care to smooth the softly curling wheat-colored hair out of her face so none of the strands were caught in her eyes or her mouth.

The binding accomplished, he stood back from her again.

It was not for him to wonder—and yet, he *did* wonder. If his liege wanted this woman effectively coaxed, why in the name of the frozen towers of Hel had he sent a soldier to do it?

The soles of her feet, turned out to him because of his perhaps too-cautious binding, seemed to reproach him. He bent, gently scooped her up and turned her so that she was facing the room again. Bound was bound and she wouldn't like it, but at least in her current position, when she woke, she could see what went on around her.

He noted a flicker of movement in his side vision, tensed, and then relaxed again. It was only those two cats he'd spotted earlier, when he'd entered the apartment. One was big and white, the other sleek and black. They were sitting side by side beneath the table in the kitchen area, watching him.

"Freyja's eyes," he muttered, and then smiled to himself. The oath was fitting. Freyja was the goddess of love and war. Her chariot was drawn by cats.

Hauk had more to accomplish before the darkness fell. He turned for the room where the princess slept.

Elli groaned and opened her eyes. She was lying on her side on her own couch, a rumbling ball of white fur in front of her face and a pillow cradling her head.

And speaking of her head—it ached. Her stomach felt queasy and her mouth...

She had a gag in her mouth! The gag was firmly tied and held her mouth open, so that her lips pressed back hard over her teeth. Her jaw hurt and her throat was dry and scratchy, the gag itself soggy with saliva.

And that wasn't all. Her arms and legs were tied, too.

"Rrreow?" The sound came from the white ball of purring fur in front of her face. Doodles put his damp kitty nose to her cheek and asked again, "Rreow?" Then he jumped to the carpet and trotted off toward the kitchen, fat white tail held high, no doubt hoping she would take the hint and get out there and dish up his dinner.

Elli groaned and yanked at the ropes that bound her. It didn't help. If anything, her struggling seemed to pull them tighter.

"It is best not to struggle, Your Highness," said a deep, calm voice from across the room. It was *him*— the Viking. He sat in the easy chair opposite her. With Doodles in the way, she hadn't seen him at first.

"Struggling only pulls the long rope tighter." His kindly tone made her yearn for something long and sharp to drive straight into his heart.

One of her suitcases waited upright beside his chair. Evidently, he'd done her packing for her.

"We'll be on our way soon, Princess. We're only waiting for darkness."

Waiting for darkness...

Well, of course they were waiting for darkness. Dragging a bound-and-gagged woman down a flight of stairs and out to a waiting vehicle wasn't something he'd be likely to get away with in the bright light of day.

He was silent, watching her, his expression implacable. She watched him right back, fury curling through her, banishing the thickheaded grogginess left over from the drug he'd used on her.

As a rule, Elli was good-natured and easygoing, not as ambitious as her older sister, Liv, not as brave and adventurous as Brit, the baby. Elli had always thought of herself as the *ordinary* one of the three of them, the one who wanted meaningful work that didn't eat up her life, a nice home to fill with love and, eventually, a good man to go through life beside her. They used to joke among themselves that Liv would run the world and Brit would thoroughly explore it. It would be up to Elli to settle down, get married and provide the world with the next generation.

Right now, though, looking at the man in the chair across from her, Elli didn't feel especially reasonable or easygoing or good-natured. She felt angry.

No. Anger was too mild a word. She felt a burning, growing rage.

How dare he? What gave him the right—to break into her home, to give her orders, to knock her out, to tie her up?

Her father?

So the Viking said.

And what gave her father the right? Her father *had* no rights when it came to her. He'd given them up twenty-plus years ago.

And even if her father still had some claim on her, no claim in the world made kidnapping acceptable. This was an outrage, a crime against basic human decency.

Elli wanted the ropes untied and the gag removed. And she wanted—had a *right*—to be untied *now*. She grunted and squirmed in her rage and fury.

And as her Viking captor had promised, the rope that bound her wrists to her ankles pulled tighter, until her heels met her hands and her body bowed outward beyond the outer edge of the couch cushions. Her right thigh cramped up. It was excruciatingly painful.

She let out a small, anguished moan and lay still, forcing herself to breathe slowly and deeply, to relax as best she could with her heels yanked up and pressed against her palms. Sweat broke out on her brow. She shut her eyes, concentrated on pulling her breath in and sending it out, *willing* the cramp in her thigh to let go.

The pain seemed to ease a little. She opened her eyes to find the Viking standing over her. She let out a muffled shriek as she saw the jet-black knife handle.

With an evil snicking sound, the slim, deadly blade sprang out. The Viking bent close—and cut the rope that held her hands and ankles together.

The relief was a fine and shining thing. She straightened her legs, the cramp in her thigh subsiding completely. And then, though she knew it was foolish in the extreme, she flung out her bound feet and tried to kick him.

He simply stepped to the side, collapsing the knife and kneeling in a smooth, swift motion to stow it in his boot. Then he stood to his height again.

"I am sorry to have bound you, Princess." He actually managed to sound regretful. "But your father's instructions are to bring you to him, whether you are willing or not. I can't have you trying to run away all the time—or shouting for help."

She made a series of urgent grunting sounds, shaking her head with each one.

He got the message. Reluctantly, he suggested, "You wish me to remove the gag."

"Umn, uhgh, umngh." She nodded madly.

"If I remove the gag, you must swear on your honor as a descendant of kings not to cry out or make any loud sounds."

She nodded again—that time sharply and firmly.

He was silent, regarding her. She stared right back at him, unmoving now, willing him with her eyes to take off the gag.

At last, he spoke. "You are a princess of the House of Thor. To you, honor should be all." His doubting expression was distinctly unflattering. "But you have been raised in...this." He gestured toward the glass door that led out to her small balcony. The sun was lowering now. A massive oak grew beyond the balcony and the sunlight shone through its branches, creating enchanting patterns of shadow and light.

The Viking sneered. "This California is an easy, warm place, far from the hard snows and misty fjords of our island home. You know nothing of the endless nights of winter. The frost giants, harbingers of Ragnarok, do not stalk your dreams. Perhaps you do not hold your honor precious above all else as you should."

Elli knew the Norse myths. She understood his references. Still, what he said sounded like something out of *Lord of the Rings*. She should have found such talk ridiculous. But she didn't. His meaning was crystal clear. He believed she wouldn't keep her word, that she'd scream her head off the second he took the gag away.

A minute ago, she had planned to do exactly that. But not anymore. Now, she would not scream if her life depended on it. Now, she was madder, even, than a minute ago. She was utterly, bone-shatteringly furious—which was thoroughly unreasonable, as he only suspected what she *had* planned to do.

But this was far from a reasonable situation. And Elli Thorson boiled with rage. She didn't move, she didn't *breathe*. She simply stared at him, her gaze burning through him, wishing she could sear him to a cinder where he stood.

Evidently, the hot fury in her eyes was the answer he sought. He stepped in front of her once more and knelt opposite her head. They shared another long look. And then he reached out and untied the gag. "Forgive me, Your Highness. I want you to be comfortable, but I must know that I can trust you."

"I don't forgive you," she muttered in a dry croak. "So stop asking me to." Elli pressed her lips together, ran her tongue over her dried-out teeth and swallowed repeatedly to soothe her parched throat. Finally, she said in a low voice, "Water. Please."

He dropped the gag on the couch arm and went to the kitchen, returning quickly with a full glass. He set the glass on the coffee table and helped her to sit. Her skirt was halfway up her thighs. He smoothed it down so it covered her tied-together knees. She had a powerful urge to snap at him to get his big, rude hands off her, but she pressed her lips together over the self-defeating words. She did want her skirt pulled down and since her own hands were tied, his would have to do.

Once she was upright, with her skirt where it was supposed to be, he held the glass to her lips. Oh, it was heaven, that lovely, wet water sliding down her dry throat. She drank the whole thing.

"More?" he asked. She shook her head. He was very close, his bulging hard shoulder brushing against her. She realized she could smell him. His skin gave off a scent both spicy and fresh. Like cloves and green, newly cut cedar boughs. Every Christmas, her mother decked the mantels and stair rails with cedar boughs. Elli had always loved the smell of them....

And what was the matter with her? Had she lost her mind?

He had drugged her and tied her up and as soon as

dark came, he was dragging her out of here, hauling her off to God knew where. The last thing she should be thinking about was how good he smelled.

She scooted as far away from him as she could, given her hobbled state, and hugged the couch arm.

Without another word, he set the empty glass on the coffee table, stood and crossed the room to sit again in the easy chair—as if he found it uncomfortable or distasteful to be anywhere near her. Fine. She felt the same way. On both counts.

Neither of them spoke for several minutes. The Viking was still. Elli fidgeted a little, pulling at the ropes that bound her, unable to resist a need to test them. Unlike the rope he had cut, the ones that were left pulled no tighter when she tugged on them. They didn't loosen, either.

It occurred to her that the only weapon she had at her disposal right then was her voice. Shouting for help was out. She'd sworn she wouldn't do that, and for some insane reason she felt bound to stick by her word. However, she'd never promised she wouldn't speak. And words, if used right, could serve as weapons.

She straightened her shoulders and let out a long breath. "This is kidnapping, do you realize that? In America, what you're doing is a capital crime."

He looked away, toward the kitchen, where both of her cats—Doodles and Diablo—sat side by side, waiting for the dinner that was so long in coming. Elli began to wonder if the Viking would reply to her.

And then that gray-blue gaze swung her way again.

"You will not be harmed. I will take you to your father. He will explain all."

A shriek of rage and frustration rose in her throat. She had to swallow to banish it. She spoke with measured care. "None of that is the point. The point is—"

He raised that tattooed palm. "Enough. I have told you what will happen. Make your peace with it."

Not in a hundred million years. "Untie me. I have to feed my cats."

He just looked at her, reproach in those watchful eyes.

Though it galled like burning acid to do it, she gave him the oath he required. "I will not try to escape—not while we're here, in my apartment. You have my word of honor on that."

He studied her some more in that probing, intense way he had, as if he knew how to look through her skull, to see into her real thoughts and know for certain if she told the truth or if she lied. Finally, he bent to his boot and removed the black knife. *Snick.* The blade appeared, gleaming.

He rose and came toward her again. She wriggled sideways, twisting from the waist, presenting her bound wrists.

He slid the knife between them. She felt the cool flat of the blade. A quick, annoying brush of his skin against hers—and the rope fell away. She brought her hands to the front and rubbed her chafed wrists.

The Viking knelt before her, golden hair flowing thick and shaggy to his huge shoulders. He slipped the knife beneath the rope that bound her ankles. His fingers whispered against the upper arch of her foot—and her ankles were free. He raised the knife, the steel glinting, and slid it between her knees, slicing the rope there, his knuckles making brief and burning contact with the inside of her leg. When he pulled the knife away, he gave it a flick. The blade disappeared. Swiftly he gathered the bits of rope and the soggy gag.

The knife went into his boot and he stood. He backed away without once looking up, got a black bag from behind the easy chair and stowed the cut ropes and the gag in it. Then he sat in the chair once more.

Only then did he look at her, his eyelids low, his gaze brooding. "Go, Princess. Feed your animals."

She stood slowly, expecting a little dizziness from the drug he'd used on her—and some stiffness from being tied up so tightly. But it wasn't bad. Her head swam at first, and her stomach lurched, but both sensations passed quickly.

Her cats jumped up and followed her as she went past, Doodles meowing at her to hurry it up, Diablo a silent shadow, taking up the rear. She dished up the food, covered the half-used can and put it back in the refrigerator. Then she rinsed the spoon and stuck it in the dishwasher.

Her apartment, in a four-building complex, was at one end of her building. She had a window over her kitchen sink. She lingered for a moment, looking across at the next building over, and down at the slopes of grass and the concrete walkway below. She saw no one right then, but she couldn't help wondering...

If she were to signal a passing neighbor, would that count as trying to escape?

"Princess."

She let out a cry—actually a guilty-sounding squeak—and jumped back from the window. The Viking was standing about eight feet away, by her table with her bags of groceries still waiting on it. Damn him. How did he do it, appear out of nowhere like that without making a sound?

Slowly, he shook that gold head at her. As if he knew exactly the question she'd been asking herself and had materialized in her kitchen to let her know that he still had a few lengths of rope handy for any naughty princess who insisted on breaking her word.

"Look," she snarled. "Do you mind if I at least put my groceries away?"

"As you wish."

Hah, she thought. None of this—*none*—was as she wished.

But she'd already made that point painfully clear to him. And he was still here and still planning to take her to Gullandria with him as soon as it got dark.

With a sigh, she went to the table and began unloading the bags. He stepped out of the way, but he didn't go back to his chair in the living room. Instead, he stood a few feet from the table, arms crossed over his chest, watching her put the lettuce and the Clearly Canadians in the refrigerator, the Grey Poupon in the cupboard.

Once she had everything put away, they returned to their respective seats in the living room.

The silence descended once more. He watched, she waited—or maybe it was the other way around. Doodles and Diablo jumped up beside her and settled in, purring. She petted them—the thick white coat, the velvety black one. There was some comfort in touching them, in feeling the soft roar of their purrs vibrating against her palm.

The phone rang, startling her. She'd been avoiding looking at him, but when she heard the shrill, insistent sound, her gaze tracked immediately to his.

"Leave it."

"But—" Before she could devise some really good reason why he had to let her answer it, it stopped— on the second ring. She wanted to shout at it, at whoever had called and given up too soon, *Damn you, can't you see I need a little help here? What's holding on for a few more rings going to cost you?*

Outside, it was still light. But it wouldn't be that long until night fell. When that happened, he'd be dragging her out of here by the hair—figuratively speaking.

Was she ready for that? Not. There had to be a better way.

She made herself look at him again—and then she forced her voice to a friendly tone. "Hauk… May I call you Hauk?"

He cleared his throat. "Call me what you will. I am—"

She waved a hand. "At my service. Got that. But Hauk?"

"Your Highness?"

Oh, this was all so way, way weird. "Look. Could you just call me Elli?"

The silver-blue gaze slid away. "That would not be appropriate."

Elli stared at his profile for a count of ten. Then she sighed. "Please. I think we have to talk." He turned those eyes on her again—but he didn't speak. When the silence had stretched out too long, she suggested, "What if I were to go with you willingly?"

His gaze was unblinking, his face a carved mask. "Then you would make the inevitable easier on everyone."

She added hopefully, "There would be conditions."

And that brought on another of those never-ending silences. Surprise, surprise, she thought. *He's not interested in my conditions.*

Gamely, she prompted, "Let me explain."

For that, she got one gold eyebrow lifted. "I need no explanations. I have my orders and I will carry them out."

"But—"

"Your Highness, all your clever words will get you nowhere."

"Clever?" She had that dangerous feeling again, the one that told her she was about to throw back her head and scream the house down. "You think I'm *clever?*"

"Don't," he said softly, and then again, in a whisper, "Don't."

She pressed her lips together hard and folded her hands in her lap, bending her head, as if in prayer.

And in a way, she *was* praying—praying that she'd figure out how to get through to the Viking in the easy chair before he tossed her over his shoulder and headed for the door.

Elli sat up straight. "Why does my father suddenly just have to see me?"

He frowned. "As I said earlier, he will explain that himself."

"But what did he tell *you*—or did he even bother to give you the order himself?"

That eyebrow inched upward again. "Are you trying to goad me, Princess?"

She opened her mouth to deny that—and then shut it before she spoke. She had a sense that to lie to this man was to lose all hope of getting anywhere with him. She said, quietly, "Yes. I was goading you." She swallowed and then made herself add, "I apologize."

He gave her an infinitesimal shrug.

She looked up at him from under her lashes, head lowered modestly, "Please. I really do want to know. Did you speak with my father yourself? Did he tell you in person to come here and get me?"

An excruciating parade of seconds went by. Finally, the Viking said, "Yes."

"And what did he *say,* when he gave you your orders?"

"I have told you what he said. That he wanted to see you, that he would explain all once you were at his side."

"But why does he want me there?"

"He didn't tell me. And there is no reason he *should* have told me. A king is not obligated to share his motives with those who serve him."

"But he must have said *something*."

Hauk had that look again, that carved-in-stone look. The one that told her she'd gotten all the information she was going to get from him.

Well, too bad. She wanted some answers. And maybe, if she handled this right, she could make him give them to her. "You've said more than once that you are at my service."

"And so I am, Princess Elli."

"Wonderful—and I want you to know, I do understand that, while you serve me, you serve my father first."

"Yes, Your Highness."

"So that would mean, if something I ask of you doesn't affect your ability to do what my father wants, you would do *my* will. You would, as you said, serve *me*." She waited. She knew, eventually, he would have to say it.

And eventually, he did. "Yes, Princess Elli."

A slow warmth was spreading through her. She knew she had him now. "And when my father gave you the order to bring me to Gullandria, did he also instruct you not to tell *me* what he had told *you*?"

"No, Princess. He didn't."

"Then, since what I ask does not conflict with my father's wishes, I want you to serve me now and tell me what my father said to you when he ordered you to come for me."

Oh, she did have him. And yes, he did know it.

He sat ramrod straight in the chair. "His Majesty's instructions were brief. I was to be…gentle with you. First, I was to ask you to come with me. I was to tell you what I *have* told you, that your father wished to see you, to speak with you, that he would explain everything once he had you with him."

She knew the rest. "And if I said no, he told you to kidnap me and bring me to him, anyway."

Hauk looked offended. "Never once did he use the word *kidnap.*"

"But that *is* what he expected—I mean, it's what you're doing. Right?" For that she got a one-shoulder shrug. She sat forward. "But why didn't he at least call me? Why couldn't he ask me himself?"

"Highness, you ask of one who has no answers. As I told you before, a king doesn't concern himself with 'whys' when giving orders to his warrior. Your father has said that all will be revealed to you in time and His Majesty is a man of his word."

"But I don't—"

"Your Highness." Those frosty blue eyes had a warning gleam in them now.

"Hmm?" She gave him bright, sweet smile.

He looked as if a series of crude Norse oaths was scrolling through his mind. He said softly, "Patience is a quality to be prized in a woman. It would serve you well to exercise a little of it."

In a pig's eye. "Think about this, Hauk. Just think about it. My father told you he would prefer that I went willingly. And I am seriously considering doing just that."

"You're considering."

"Yes. I am. I truly am."

He might be the strong, silent type, but he wasn't any fool. He knew where this was headed. He said bleakly, "You're considering, but there is a condition."

"That's right. And it's a perfectly reasonable one. I want you to call my father and let me talk to him."

Chapter Three

She wanted to talk to her father.

Hauk couldn't believe it. The woman was too wily by half. She'd led him in circles until she had him right where she wanted him—with his head spinning. And then she'd made the one demand he wasn't sure he could refuse.

It was removing the gag that had done it. He never should have made such a fool's move. But his lord had tied his hands—as surely as Hauk had tied *hers*.

Bring her, but do it gently. Coax her, but use force if you must.

The instructions were a tangle of foggy contradictions. And that put Hauk in the position of abducting her—and also having to listen to whatever she had to say.

The cursed woman was still talking. "Hauk, come

on. I know you have to have a way to get in touch with him—a beeper? A phone number? A hotline to Isenhalla? It's so simple, don't you see? I want you to call the number, or whatever it is, and let me speak with my father.''

Hauk didn't know what to do, so he did nothing. He sat still in the chair and said not a word.

Silence and stillness didn't save him. Princess Elli rattled on. ''My father wants me to come to him, period. But first and foremost, he hopes I'll come to him voluntarily. And that's perfectly understandable that he would want that—any father would, after all. And if a phone call will do that, will make me agree to go, then wouldn't it be my father's will that you call him and let me speak with him?''

Why wouldn't the infernal woman shut up? Though Hauk had never before questioned the actions of his king, how, by the ravens of Odin, could he help but question them now?

The king's orders echoed in his head. First *ask* the woman to come—and then force her if she refuses. And don't forget—be gentle about it.

The king must have believed that she *would* refuse, or else why send his warrior to get her? Perhaps if she'd had need of a bodyguard...

But there had been no mention of an outside threat. Therefore, if His Majesty had truly believed the girl might come willingly, he would have chosen someone other than a fighting man to fetch her, someone with a honeyed tongue, someone who knew how to coax and cajole, someone who could outtalk the woman sitting opposite him now.

"First and foremost," the irritating princess repeated for at least the tenth time, "he wanted me to *want* to come. So what could it cost you to call? Nothing. But if you *don't* call, and later my father learns that all I wanted to come voluntarily was a chance to—"

"All right."

Elli couldn't believe her ears. Was he saying what she thought he was saying? Had she actually gotten through to him? She gaped at him. "Uh. You mean, you will? You'll call him?"

He had that black bag right beside him. He reached into it and pulled out a small electronic device—it looked like some kind of beeper. He punched some buttons on the face of the thing, stared at it for maybe fifteen seconds and tucked it back in the bag.

And then he straightened in the chair and stared straight ahead.

Elli couldn't stand it. "What did you just do? What is happening?"

He waited a nerve-shattering count of five before he answered, "I have contacted your father. Unless something unexpected keeps him from it, he will be calling here within the hour."

Forty-three minutes later, the phone rang. Elli leaped to her feet at the sound, jostling the cats, who shot from the couch and streaked off down the hall.

"Wait," the Viking commanded.

"But I—"

"Stay where you are."

Every nerve in her body thrumming with excruciating anticipation, Elli stayed put. The Viking went to the phone. He checked the call waiting display and then picked it up. "FitzWyborn here…yes, my lord. She is here. She has agreed to come with me, on the condition that she might speak to you first. Yes, my lord. As you will." Hauk held out the phone to her. "Your father will speak with you, Princess Elli."

Elli could not move.

That bizarre feeling of unreality had returned, freezing her where she stood. Surely this was all a dream. The father she had never known couldn't actually be on the other end of that line. And, now that she thought about it, how could she possibly be certain that the man waiting to speak with her wasn't an imposter? Hauk said the caller was her father, but his saying it didn't necessarily make it so.

The Viking strode toward her. When he reached her, he opened his hand. On top of the blue-and-gold lightning bolt lay her phone. She took it, put it to her ear.

"Hello?" It came out sounding awful, whispery and weak.

"Elli." The voice on the other end was gentle and deep. "Little Old Giant," the voice said, so tenderly.

Little Old Giant. Nobody called her that. Nobody. Except her mother, when she was a child…

"You're my Little Old Giant, Elli, that's what you are."

"No, Mommy. I'm not a giant. I'm way too small."

"But your name is a myth name. A name from the old, old stories that are told in the land where you were born."

"In Gullandria, Mommy?"

"That's right. In Gullandria. And in Gullandria, they tell the story of Elli, the giantess. Elli was a very old giantess—so old, she was old age itself. The Thunder god, Thor, was tricked into fighting her, though everyone knows…"

"You can't fight old age," Elli said softly into the phone.

Her father—and she knew it was her father now—laughed. He had a good, strong laugh. A kind laugh, warm and sure. He said, "Ah. Your mother has taught you something, at least, of who you are."

Elli felt the tears. They burned behind her eyes, pushed at the back of her throat. Hauk had returned to his chair, but his ice-blue gaze was on her.

She looked away, dashed at her damp eyes and asked her father, "If you wanted to see me, why did you have to do it this way?"

"I need you to come, Elli. Please. Come with Hauk. *Trust* Hauk. He will never harm you and he will keep you safe. Let him bring you to me."

"Father." So strange. To be speaking to him, at last, after all these years. "You haven't answered my question."

There was a silence from the other end of the line. Elli heard static, in the background, thought of the thousands of miles of distance between her life, here, at home in Sacramento and her father, on the island of her birth in the Norwegian Sea. What time was it there? Late at night, she thought. Was he in bed as he talked to her, or fully dressed in some high-ceilinged study or huge palace drawing room?

He spoke again. "I have lost two sons. Is it so very strange that I would yearn to meet at last a daughter of my blood?"

"But why didn't you just call me, ask me?"

"Would you have said yes?"

It was a question she couldn't have answered five minutes ago—but that was before she heard his sad, kind voice calling her by the special name only he and her mother knew.

"I would have," she said firmly. "In a heartbeat, I would have said yes."

Hearing his voice did not, by any means, make everything all right. There remained great hurt in her heart, and bitterness, too. He had, after all, treated her and her sisters as disposable children. She knew something terrible had happened, all those years ago, between him and her mother, to make them carve their family in two, to send her mother fleeing back home to America with her three baby princesses, leaving her sons behind. Elli and her sisters had tried, over and over, to find out what had caused the awful rift. But their mother would not say.

Elli turned again toward the Viking sitting in her easy chair. She gave him her most defiant stare. Really, what was this crazy kidnapping plot of her father's, if not his misguided way of fighting for a chance to make things right in their family at last? She *wanted* to go now, to meet her father face-to-face, to see the land of her birth. As it stood now, Hauk would have had to lock her up and throw away the key to *keep* her from going.

Her father said dryly, "Perhaps I was in error, not to call first."

"You certainly were," she chided him. "And what about Liv and Brit? Are you having them kidnapped, too?"

"No, Elli." She could hear the humor in his voice. "Only you."

"Why only me?"

He chuckled. "As a baby, you had curious eyes. I see some things haven't changed."

"So far, you're just like this refugee from the WWE you sent here to strong-arm me." She glared all the harder at Hauk and then accused into the phone, "You keep evading all my questions."

"Come to me. You will know all."

"That's what *he* keeps saying." *He* didn't so much as blink. He was doing what he always did, sitting utterly still, staring steadily back at her.

Her father coaxed in her ear, "Elli, I do long to see your face, to talk with you at length, to get to know you, at least a little...."

Her throat closed up again. She swallowed. "I said I would come. I meant it."

"Good then."

"But first—"

Even through the static, she heard her father sigh. "I don't think I like the sound of that."

"Father, be reasonable. I can't just...disappear. I have a life and my life deserves consideration. I have to get someone to feed my cats and water my plants. I have to call my principal at school, arrange for some family leave. And I have to see Mom and tell her—"

''Not your mother.'' Her father's voice was suddenly cold as the steel blade of Hauk's knife. ''Absolutely no.'' It was a command.

Too bad. ''There is no way I'm disappearing without explaining to her what I'm doing. She would be frantic, terrified for me. I could never put her through something like that.''

''If Ingrid knows where you're going she'll never allow it.''

''You don't know that for certain—and besides, Mom doesn't tell me what I can or can't do.''

''I do know for certain. I've already approached her on this issue. She flatly refused me.''

That was news to Elli—big news. ''You spoke with Mom about my coming to see you?''

''I did.''

''When?''

''A few days ago.''

''You…you *called* her? On the phone?''

''I did.''

''But you two haven't spoken in—''

''A very long time.''

''She hasn't said a word to me about it.''

''I don't find that in the least surprising.'' Her father's voice wasn't as icy as a moment ago—but there remained a distinct chill in it.

''I don't understand.''

''It's quite simple. I called your mother. I asked that she send you and your sisters for a visit. She refused. I tried to get through to her. I pointed out that I'm your father, that I've waited all these years and I have a right to know my daughters. She wouldn't listen. She told me that you and your sisters wanted nothing to do with me, that I was to leave you alone and stay out of your lives. And then she hung up on me."

Elli knew for certain now that she wouldn't leave Sacramento before she'd had a serious talk with her mother. "Father." The word still felt strange in her mouth. "I'm an adult, past the age when my mother decides what I can or can't do. I make my own plans. And I plan to come and visit you. It's Monday night. Give me two days. By Thursday morning at the latest, I will be on a plane, on my way to Gullandria." She added, with a meaningful glance at the Viking sitting still as a statue across from her, "You have my word of honor on that."

There was a silence on the other end. Even the static stopped. And then her father said thoughtfully, "Your word of honor…"

"Yes. My word of honor."

"Put Hauk on."

She felt irritation rising. "Why do you need to talk to—"

"Please, Elli. Put him on."

Elli marched over to the Viking. "Here. Tell him my word of honor can be trusted."

He took the phone. "Yes, my lord…yes…yes, I do…" He listened. His face remained expressionless, but something in the set of his jaw told her he didn't much care for whatever he was hearing. "Yes, Your Majesty," he said at last and gave her the phone back.

She spoke to her father again. "Satisfied?"

Her father answered calmly. "I think we have an agreement."

"We do?"

"That's right, my daughter. Speak with your mother if you must. And be on that plane by Thursday morning."

Elli smiled. "Great. Thank you, Father. I'm looking forward to seeing you at last."

"And I'm looking forward to seeing *you*." His voice was tender again. "So very much." Then he added offhandedly, "Hauk will stay with you. He'll see you safely to my side."

The Viking was still staring at her. Elli spun away from him, stalked back to the couch and plunked down onto it. She sent a fulminating glance across the room before she muttered into the phone, "You have my word. There's no need for—"

"Elli. He stays with you." Her father's tone was flat. Final.

She could speak flatly, too. "You know what this tells me, Father? You don't trust my word."

His tone softened and acquired a wheedling note. "Humor an old man. Please."

Her father was in his early fifties. Old, by Elli's standards—but not *that* old. "Oh, stop. I know you're working me."

"This is one point on which I cannot back down." He was all firmness again. "Accept it. You will have the time you want to do whatever you say needs doing—including visiting your mother. But Hauk will not leave your side until he's delivered you safely into my presence."

"You think Mom is going to talk me out of coming, don't you?"

"I do."

"She won't. I swear it."

"Better safe than sorry. I do, after all, know your mother."

She looked across at Hauk again. Till Thursday—and beyond—with him right there, watching, every time she turned around. "I'm really not happy about this."

"It's my only condition." He said it as if it were a tiny thing—something so inconsequential, it meant next to nothing. "Accept it and we'll find ourselves in perfect agreement."

Elli said goodbye to her father and immediately called her mother. She made that call brief. She wanted to speak to Ingrid in person about her trip—and about the call Ingrid had received from her father, the one Ingrid had failed to mention up till now.

"Are you all right?" her mother asked. "You seem...pensive."

Elli glanced across the room. Hauk was still there, in the chair, looking on.

Might as well get used to it, she told herself. She reassured her mother that she was fine and made a date with her—dinner at Ingrid's house in Land Park the next night.

After her mother, Elli managed to reach her principal at home. She spoke—somewhat vaguely—of a family emergency, said she had to leave within a couple of days. Her boss was far from pleased. Elli was in her first year with her own classes and didn't have a lot of leave built up.

He said that yes, he would call the district for her and get someone to start tomorrow. Then he asked the logical question, "How long will you be gone?"

Unreality smacked her flat again. She hadn't even considered how long her trip might last.

But it couldn't be *that* long. It was a visit. A visit lasted... "Three weeks," she said, getting up and going to have a look at her kitchen calendar. "I'll be back and in my classroom by the twenty-seventh." At least that way, she'd be there for the final two weeks of school. She reassured him that her lesson plans were all in good order. The substitute should have no trouble figuring things out. But should a problem arise, Elli would be in town for a day or two. The sub could give her a call.

Somewhat grouchily, her boss wished her well. She realized, as she hung up the phone, that this trip could possibly cost her her job.

Elli was fortunate, and she knew it. She didn't need the money. Her mother was, after all, a Freyasdahl. And anyone with any awareness of who was who in California knew that being a Freyasdahl meant you had money—and lots of it. Elli could live quite comfortably on the proceeds from her trust. But she loved teaching and she took pride in her work. It bothered her to think she was letting her school—and especially her two classes of kindergartners—down.

She glanced over, saw Hauk again, huge, bemuscled and implacable.

Well. She'd made a promise and she would keep it. Might as well put a bright face on it.

She flashed the Viking a big, fake smile. Those golden brows drew together and he looked at her sideways, his chiseled face set in suspicious lines.

"Tell you what," she said, so cheerfully it grated on her *own* nerves. "You just make yourself right at home." She dared to get close enough to grab her suitcase from where it waited, upright, beside him. "And if you don't mind, I think I'd prefer to do my packing for myself." She turned and marched away from him down the hall.

In her bedroom, she hoisted the suitcase onto the bed. She left it there, unopened, and went into her bathroom, where she took care to engage the privacy lock.

She planned to use the toilet, but somehow she found herself leaning over the sink, staring at herself in the mirror. Her eyes looked huge and haunted. Her face was too pale, except for the cartoon-red splotches of hectic color high on her cheeks.

"I want to go and meet my father," she told her slightly stupefied reflection. "I *want* to do this." At the same time, she was still having serious trouble believing any of it was really happening. Not long ago, she'd been carrying her groceries up the stairs, humming a tune that had been playing on the radio in the car, thinking about what she'd fix for dinner.

Now everything was changed. She was going to Gullandria.

She used the toilet, washed her hands, brushed her

hair and got another long, cool drink of water from the tap. She put on fresh lip gloss.

And then she went out to face the Viking—which happened sooner than she expected, as she found him standing beside her bed.

She shrieked in outrage. "Get out!"

"Princess, it is not my intention to frighten you."

It was too much—him here, in her bedroom. She made shooing motions with both hands and shouted, "Out, out, out!"

"Silence!" he boomed back, then reminded her, way too softly, "Remember your promise. No loud noises."

She lowered her voice to a furious whisper. "That was before, when you were kidnapping me. Now you are merely my...escort. And I want you out of my room."

Instead of leaving, he came toward her. Those huge, heavily muscled legs were so long, it only took about a step and a half.

She wasn't afraid of him—she *wasn't*. But she couldn't stop herself from shrinking out of his path when faced with all that size and power coming right at her. He was so tall that the hair at the crown of his head brushed the top of the doorframe as he entered her bathroom.

She moved into the doorway behind him, folding her arms across her middle to keep her fists from punching something. "What in God's name are you doing?"

He didn't even bother to answer her, just started checking things out, opening the slatted pebbled-glass window and peering down at the carports, looking in her cabinets at her towels and extra bars of soap, sweeping back the shower curtain to view the tub.

"What, you think I've got someone hidden in the tub? You think I'm planning to bust out—just take all the slats out of that window and jump onto the hood of somebody's Jetta? Oh, puh-lease."

Apparently, he had finished his invasion of her privacy, because he stood still, facing her. "My orders are to guard you closely, Princess—to stay at your side at all times, to see that you don't change your mind about your agreement with His Majesty. I'm doing that and only that. You came in here very quickly. I felt it wise to find out if there was some reason for your haste."

"I came in here quickly because I had to go to the bathroom. Is that a problem for you, if I go to the bathroom?"

"No, Princess." He stood with that huge chest thrust out, shoulders back, his arms tight to his sides, a soldier at attention.

"And let's back up here for a minute. Is that really what my father told you, to…*guard me closely, to stay at my side all the time?*"

"Yes, Princess."

"I think I'm going to have to talk to my father again."

The Viking didn't move.

"Did you hear me? I said, contact my father again. I wish to speak with him."

"I'm sorry, Your Highness. I can't do that."

"Sure you can. Just go get that beeper thingy and—"

"Princess."

"What?"

"Your father told me he didn't wish to be disturbed again. He said he was certain you'd think of an endless list of new questions as soon as you hung up the phone. He told me to tell you he would answer them all—"

She knew the rest. "When I see him in Gullandria."

"That is correct, Prin—"

"Hauk."

"Yes, your—"

"If you call me princess—or Your Highness—one more time, I think I'm going to forget all about my promise and my honor and start screaming. Then you'll have to tie me up again and that will make me very, very angry. And you don't really want me angry, now, do you?"

"No, P—" He caught himself just in time. "No."

"Well, all right then. Don't call me Your Highness and don't call me princess."

"As you wish."

"And now, will you please get out of my bedroom?"

"If you'll come with me."

She threw up both hands. "All right, all right. Let's go."

Elli went straight to the kitchen. It was almost eight by then and her stomach was making insistent growling sounds.

Of course, Hauk followed right behind her. That was okay, she supposed. She'd resigned herself to feeding him, too.

"Sit down," she told him and threw out a hand in the direction of the table. "Over there."

He took the chair that put his back to the wall. He could see down the hall and into the living room and, of course, he had a clear view of her activities in the kitchen. The man certainly took his duties seriously. How did he do it? So much watchfulness had to wear a person out.

She pulled open the refrigerator and stared at the chicken she'd brought home to roast. It would be enough for both of them, but it would also take almost two hours in the oven.

No. She was hungry *now*.

She considered a quick trip to Mickey D's or Taco Bell.

But then again, it wasn't as if she'd be allowed to just jump in her car and go. The king's warrior would have to be consulted. They'd have to wrangle over whether she could go at all. Then, if he allowed it, he'd insist on going with her. He'd decide who would drive—she was betting on herself. That way he'd have his hands free to deal with her if she broke her word and tried to leap to freedom from the moving vehicle. Then there'd be the question of whether she could actually be trusted to speak to the order taker at the drive-up window....

Uh-uh. Fast food was a no-go.

Elli tried the freezer. Ah. A pair of DiGiornos. Perfect. She glanced at the huge man in her kitchen chair again and decided she'd better cook both the three-meat *and* the deluxe.

When she set a plate before him, he frowned. "It is not necessary that you cook for me."

And what was he planning to eat if she didn't?

Better not even get into it. "It's nothing fancy—pizza and a salad. Just eat it, okay?"

He dipped his shaggy golden head. "Thank you, Pr—" He stifled the P-word, barely. "Uh. Thank you."

"You're welcome."

She had a nice bottle of chardonnay chilling. She'd grabbed it at the supermarket, thinking she'd have a glass with her roast chicken. She decided to open it now. She needed *something* to help get her through the night.

Elli set out two glasses, but when she tried to pour one for Hauk, he put his great big hand over the mouth of it. Well, fine, she thought. Be that way. More for me. She filled her own glass to the brim and sat opposite him. They ate in silence. Elli indulged in a second glass of wine.

She was feeling pleasantly hazy when she got up to put the dishes in the dishwasher. Hauk rose with her. He helped her clear off, and actually took the sponge and began wiping the counters as she rinsed the plates and put them in the dishwasher. She turned and looked at him, sponging her table, carefully guiding the pizza crumbs into his massive paw of a hand—and she couldn't help it. A goofy giggle escaped her.

He straightened—still holding the crumbs cupped in his hand—and turned to her. "You find me humorous?"

"I...uh..." She waved a hand. "Never mind. It's nothing."

He came toward her. Maybe it was the wine, but for the first time, she didn't feel particularly menaced by the sight of all that muscle moving her way. She stepped back a fraction, so he could brush the crumbs into the sink. Then she took the spray attachment and rinsed them down the drain. He handed her the sponge. She rinsed it, wrung the water from it and set it in the wire basket under the sink.

"Well," she said. "That's that."

He nodded. And then he just stood there—awaiting orders, she supposed.

It was 8:50. A little early for bed under ordinary circumstances. But ordinary had nothing at all to do with tonight. She wanted some time to herself, for Pete's sake, a few hours without the ever-watchful eyes of the king's warrior tracking her every move. And the only way to get that was to say good-night and shut her bedroom door.

"Listen." She tried a smile on him.

He gave her another nod.

She told him, "I'm just going to make up the futon in the spare room for you. You'll find fresh towels in the cabinet to the right of the sink in the hall bathroom. And if you want to watch a little television, the living room is all yours—oh, and if you get hungry, hey, if I've got it, you can eat it."

He just stood there, looking at her. She knew with absolute certainty he had something to tell her that she wasn't going to like.

"What?" she demanded.

"Your intention is that I sleep in your extra room and you sleep in your own bedroom."

"Something wrong with that?"

"It appears you haven't clearly understood the agreement you made with His Majesty."

She backed up a step, slapped a hand down on the counter tiles and glared at him sideways. "What are you talking about? I agreed to go visit him. I agreed that you could hang around in my apartment until it's time to go, keeping an eye on me so I won't change my mind. I agreed that you would be my escort to Gullandria."

"Yes, all that is correct."

"Good. So we know what I agreed to. And I'm going to bed." She moved forward. He *didn't* move aside. "Hauk. If you don't tell me what is going on here…" She let the threat trail off, mostly because she couldn't think of anything sufficiently terrible to threaten him *with*.

"All right," he growled. He looked especially bleak right then. "His Majesty instructed me to watch over you at all times. That means wherever you sleep, I sleep as well."

Chapter Four

"That's the most ridiculous thing I ever heard," the princess announced. "I never agreed to sleep with you. My father never said a word about my sleeping with you." She shook her head as if to clear it. "Why would my father want me to sleep with you?"

Hauk realized she'd drawn an erroneous conclusion. "Of course you would not sleep *with* me. But whatever room you sleep in—I will be there, also."

She blinked, and then she said, very slowly, "You think you're going to sleep in my room."

"It is of no consequence to me what room I sleep in. I'm merely informing you that it will be the same room as the room in which you sleep."

"But I don't... Did he *say* that to you, did he actually say you had to sleep in the same room with me?"

"He said not to let you out of my sight."

"Ah." She slapped the counter again. "But you did, remember? You let me out of your sight when I went to the bathroom and nothing happened. I'm still here."

By the runes, he hated arguing with this woman. She was too clever by half. "You have a right to your privacy, when it comes to...private matters. But not for hours. There are windows in every room. Given time, you could easily find a way to escape without my knowing it."

"But I *won't* escape. I gave you my word that I wouldn't."

"And I am ordered by my king to make certain that you keep your word."

Those proud slim shoulders slumped. She looked away. "I'm not going to win this one, am I?"

He wanted to say, *No, Your Highness.* But she had forbidden him the use of her title.

He also wanted to say he regretted this—all of it. But she had ordered him to stop apologizing.

And he might as well admit she was right—not about his addressing her properly. He didn't like the familiarity she was forcing on him by making him drop the appropriate form of address. But as to his regrets, well, they had no more value than a promise made by Loki, the god of dirty tricks.

It was what a man did that mattered, not what came out of his mouth. And what Hauk would do was continue to follow the orders of his king.

She asked, sounding forlorn, "Will you at least leave me alone while I take a bath?"

Hauk allowed her the bath.

But she couldn't relax. She lay in the scented water, thinking of the huge man waiting on the other side of the door, knowing that if she stayed in there too long, he'd be busting in to see what trouble she'd gotten into now. After ten minutes or so, before the water even started to cool, she got out, toweled dry, pulled on her pink sleep shirt, and quickly brushed her teeth.

He was waiting in the middle of her bedroom. He'd found some blankets and a pillow and laid them out on the carpet at the foot of her bed. Her suitcase was still there, on the bed where she'd tossed it, full of whatever he'd chosen to put in it while she lay, drugged and bound, on the couch in the living room.

"I took bedding from your closet in the hallway," he said, his head tipped down, as if he expected a reprimand.

Who cared if the man borrowed a blanket? He could borrow a hundred blankets—if he'd only take them in the spare room to sleep on them.

Elli crossed her arms over her chest—a gesture of self-protection. All of a sudden, she felt way too naked, though her sleep shirt was baggy and reached almost to her knees. She stared at the Viking, biting her lip.

Maybe she could bear it, having him in her bedroom all night, if he wasn't quite so...masculine. He was very controlled, but still testosterone seemed to ooze from every pore. And then there were all those hard, bulging muscles...

Elli hugged herself tighter and looked away from him. She stared at her suitcase.

He must have noted the direction of her gaze. "You wish to do your packing now?"

A shiver slid beneath the surface of her skin. It was all so eerie. He was her jailer. And yet, at the same time, he behaved like a loyal servant, ready to do her bidding before she even told him what her bidding was.

"No, I'll do it later. I have until Thursday, remember?" It was something of a dig. Even if he *had* almost kidnapped her, he seemed, at heart, a noble, straight-ahead kind of guy. He probably didn't like sleeping at the foot of her bed any more than she liked having him there. No doubt he hoped she'd make their time in forced proximity as short as possible, that she'd be ready to head for Gullandria as soon as she'd had that talk with her mother—tomorrow night, or Wednesday morning at the latest.

Well, okay. Maybe she *would* be ready to leave before Thursday. And maybe it would please him to know that. But pleasing the Viking in her bedroom was the last thing on her mind right then.

Stone-faced as usual, he lifted the suitcase off the bed and carried it over to set it against the wall. She smelled toothpaste as he went past. Sometime during her too-short, not-at-all-relaxing bath, he must have brushed his teeth.

What a truly odd image: the Viking in her guest bath, with a toothbrush in his mouth, scrubbing away. Somehow, when she thought of Vikings, she never imagined them brushing their teeth. Did he floss, as well? She supposed he must. Everything about him shouted physical fitness. He had to be proactive when it came to his health. Proper dental hygiene would be part of the package.

He marched by her again and returned to stand at attention near his pallet of blankets. "Do you wish to sleep now?"

As if. "In a minute. First, I need to lock up."

Before she could turn for the door, he said, "I've already done that."

"Surprise, surprise." She went to the bed and slid under the covers. Doodles and Diablo, with that radar cats seem to have for the moment when their human has settled into a soft, inviting place, appeared in the doorway to the hall. "Well, come on," she told them, and reached for the remote, which waited on her nightstand.

The cats settled in. She turned on the TV in the corner—okay, Feng Shui, it wasn't. But Elli didn't care. She loved to watch TV in bed with her cats cuddled close around her.

And a favorite program was in progress. *Law and Order: Criminal Intent.* Vincent D'Onofrio had the perp in the interrogation room and was psyching him out with skill and subtlety.

And the Viking was still standing there—awaiting orders, she supposed.

"Hauk. Go to bed."

He nodded and dropped to his blankets. A minute later, he was stretched out beneath the top blanket, his boots and belt a foot or two away. She wondered briefly where he kept that black switchblade knife when he slept—but then she told herself that where Hauk FitzWyborn kept his knife was no concern of hers. She watched the rest of her program, and after that turned to an old movie on TCM.

At the foot of the bed, Hauk lay utterly still. She could swear he hadn't moved since he crawled beneath the blanket over an hour ago.

When the movie ended, Elli switched off the television. The room seemed so very quiet. She could hear Doodles purring—and nothing else.

Could the Viking have died?

Hah. No such luck.

Had he fallen asleep? It certainly seemed that way.

What a thrilling development. Hauk. Dead to the world. Dreaming whatever a Viking warrior dreamed, and for once—since the moment she'd walked in her door that afternoon—not guarding her.

Why, she might do anything. She might get up and go in the kitchen all by herself. Might walk out on the balcony and look up at the stars. Might go down the steps and along the walk and get in her car and...go for a drive.

And not to run away, not to break her word. Oh, no. Simply because she *could*.

She'd return later, after he woke and found her gone. He would be frantic. Old stone face. Freaking out.

Ah, yes. How lovely...

Elli rearranged the cats a little, pushing them gently to the side so they wouldn't be disturbed when she slid from the bed. Then she switched off the lamp and lay back to wait awhile. She could see the glowing numerals on her bedside digital alarm clock. She'd wait half an hour. And if she still heard nothing, she was out of here.

Okay, maybe it was pointless and a little bit childish. But this whole situation deeply offended her. To show that she *could* leave if she wanted to would be something of an object lesson—to Hauk, and by extension, to her father. And maybe, if she left and came back of her own accord, Hauk would realize it wasn't necessary to take the orders of his king so literally. Maybe, by tomorrow night, she'd have her bedroom to herself.

The time passed slowly. She used it to consider her next move. Should she creep to the foot of the bed and have a look at him, see if he truly was in lullaby land?

Uh-uh. No point in tempting fate—not to mention squeaky bedsprings. Better just to ease out from under the covers and tiptoe to the door. If it turned out he'd been lying there for hours, stone still and awake, she'd find out soon enough.

The minutes crawled by. There was nothing but silence from the man at the foot of her bed.

At last, that endless half hour was behind her.

Slowly, so *quietly,* Elli eased back the covers. In one careful, unbroken move, she swung her feet out and over the edge of the bed. She slid her weight onto them without a single spring creaking. Doodles, sound asleep by then, didn't even open an eye. Diablo lifted his sleek head, blinked at her, then laid his head down again.

Good. Perfect. Wonderful.

Elli turned and started for the door to the hall. She was utterly silent. She wasn't even *breathing*. She made it into the open doorway.

"Where are you going?"

Elli gasped and whirled to face him. He was standing beside his blankets, watching her. She could have sworn he had never moved, never so much as *stirred*.

She gulped. "Uh, well…ice water! You know, I really want some ice water."

The big golden head dipped once—in permission, in acknowledgment, in who the heck knew what? Elli yanked her shoulders back and headed for the kitchen. She heard nothing behind her. But she didn't have to turn and look to know that he had followed.

Eventually, very late in the night, she finally dropped off to sleep. She woke after daylight to the sound of birds twittering in the forest: her alarm clock. Brit had given it to her a couple of Christmases ago. It made nature sounds instead of beeping or buzzing. Elli reached over and punched the off button. The cats were already off the bed and racing down the hall.

And the Viking…

All she could see from the head of the bed was the edge of his blankets. "Uh, Hauk?"

No answer.

He'd proven last night that he could hear her even if she didn't make a sound. So he must be up, or he would have answered. She pushed back the covers and scrambled to the bottom of the bed, where she found his blankets neatly folded, his pillow on top of the stack.

Boots, belt and man were gone.

Could it be? Had he really left—due to second thoughts on her father's part, maybe? Had Osrik beeped him late in the night, told Hauk to back off, that his daughter had given her word and the king had decided to trust her to find her way to Gullandria on her own?

The idea warmed her heart. Her father had faced a basic truth, apparently. He'd seen that in order to begin healing the awful breach in their family, he must *trust,* first and foremost, he must—

"You called for me?"

Hauk stood in the doorway to the hall, barechested, a half beard of shaving cream frothed over one sculpted cheek. She couldn't help gaping at his shoulders and arms, so big and hard, the muscles bulging and taut, the skin so tan and perfect, except for the occasional white ridge of scar tissue.

And his chest...

It was covered with beautiful, savage tattoos.

A lightning bolt like the one in his right palm, only much bigger, zigzagged across his bulging pectorals. Dragons and vines twisted and twined around it—and around the sword and dagger tattooed above and below it. The tail of the largest dragon trailed down his solar plexus to his navel.

His belly took her breath away. She'd never seen one like it—at least not outside of ab-machine infomercials and superhero video games.

Elli gulped and dragged her gaze up to meet those

watching eyes. "Uh. Yes." Carefully, tugging on her sleep shirt that had ridden up much too high, she rocked back so she sat on her knees. She tipped her chin to a proud angle and tried to look dignified, though she knew her cheeks were tomato-red. "I...didn't see you," she stuttered lamely. "I was wondering where you'd gone."

He lifted an eyebrow and held up a thoroughly modern cartridge-type razor. She stared at it for a moment, thinking that it looked toylike and strange in his big hand. But what had she expected, that he'd shave with his black-handled knife?

"As you see, I am here. Anything else?"

"No. That's all." She gave him a backhanded wave of dismissal. "Go on and, uh, finish up."

Elli dressed and made breakfast for both of them. Once they'd cleared off the table, she returned to the bedroom, Hauk close behind. He sat in the corner chair as she unpacked her suitcase.

When she was finished, she set it, empty, back against the wall.

"When will you pack?"

She looked at him, surprised to hear his voice. He'd said hardly a word since she'd called him, half-shaved, from the bathroom earlier. "I'll get to it. I have plenty of time."

He didn't say anything more, but she knew he didn't like it, that it bugged him, big-time, to think she might insist on hanging around in Sacramento till the last possible minute on Thursday. Baby-sitting a princess was not his idea of a good time and he wanted to get it over and done with, ASAP.

Too bad. Let him be bugged. Let him wait and wonder when she would end their constant togetherness and agree to get on the plane for Gullandria. It might be petty—really, really *small* of her, to torture him when he was only following orders.

But he ought to know better than to follow such orders as the ones her father had given him. He ought to stand up and say, *My lord, I'm taking a pass on playing watchdog to your daughter. It's beneath me and beneath her and I'm not going to do it.*

He hadn't said that, or anything like it. So let him sleep at the foot of her bed and stand by the bathroom door whenever she went in there and march along beside her if she dared to go outside. Served him right, as far as she was concerned.

Elli called a girlfriend, Barb Ferris, at the insurance office where Barb worked. She made that call on speakerphone, at Hauk's insistence that he be able to hear both sides of her conversation.

Barb agreed to water Elli's plants, to bring in her mail and newspapers and keep an eye on her apartment. Barb even offered to feed Doodles and Diablo, but Elli said she'd get back to her on that. She was hoping to get her mother to take the cats. Barb said sure, she'd tell the other girls that Elli was taking off for a few weeks and would miss their girls' night out on Friday. When Barb asked her what was up, Elli said it was a family issue.

"Honest, Barb. It's nothing too serious. I'll be back in three weeks. Thanks a bunch for helping me out."

Next, Elli called Ned Handly, her date for Saturday night. Ned was a doctor, in family practice. They'd met through a mutual friend and Saturday would have been their second date. Hauk stood a couple of feet away, wearing his usual carved-granite expression, as she told Ned she was going away for a while.

Ned said, with real regret, "I was looking forward to this weekend."

Elli glared at Hauk. You'd think he'd have the courtesy to let her break her date in peace. But no. He had to loom right beside her, listening to every word, every disappointed sigh.

"I was, too," Elli told Ned. "I hope you'll give me a rain check."

"I thought you'd never ask. A family trip, huh?" Elli had given him no details—and not because the stone-faced Viking standing next to her might not approve. News like this would travel fast, and she wanted to be the one to break it to her mother.

Her friends often used her title teasingly, calling her "the princess," and "Your Highness." They all thought she was so wonderfully *unusual,* one of three triplet princesses, her estranged father a king in some faraway northern land. As soon as one of them heard she was off for a visit to Gullandria, they'd burn up the phone lines sharing the scoop. Her mother might get wind of it before tonight. Someone might even let something drop to the tabloids.

Then the stinky stuff would really hit the fan.

So she was keeping the details to herself. "Yes, a family thing. But I'll give you a call as soon as I get back."

"Elli?"

"Hmm?"

"You take care."

"I will." She disconnected the call and wrinkled her nose at the big guy in black. "Well, now, wasn't that innocuous and aren't you glad you heard every word?"

Hauk said nothing. He just stood there, waiting for her to make her next move.

She realized she didn't *have* a move. No one had called from the school or the district, so presumably the sub had been contacted and was, at that moment, teaching Elli's morning class, managing just fine with the lesson plans Elli had left open on her desk.

Except for packing and dealing with her mother, Elli was ready to go.

And it was only ten in the morning—ten in the morning on *Tuesday*. She looked at Hauk, who gazed steadily back at her.

Elli sighed. "Oh, Hauk. What in the world am I going to do with you?"

"Pack your belongings," he suggested softly. "His Majesty's jet awaits you. As soon as you've spoken with your mother, we can be on our way."

Chapter Five

Elli didn't pack. Her father had agreed to give her till Thursday and, for the time being anyway, she was keeping that option open. She wasn't sure why. Maybe it was simply because, with Hauk shadowing her every move, it felt like the only option she had.

She went to the spare room, where she kept her computer. Hauk sat at attention on her futon while she surfed the Net for a while and fiddled with e-mail. Then, for an hour or so, she made a valiant effort to get a little reading done.

But it was no good. She kept feeling those cool, careful eyes on her. She couldn't concentrate on a book.

They had lunch at one. By then she was aching for a little ordinary conversation. Over BLTs she tried to engage him in a nice, friendly chat.

He was the master of the one-line reply. He'd get it down to a single word if he could, or better still, a low, unpromising sound in his throat. She got a number of curt noes, a lonely little yes or two and a whole lot of gruff grunts.

Finally, she asked him about his family. "Do you have brothers—or sisters?"

"No."

"And your mother and father?"

He just looked at her.

"Your parents, are they still alive?"

"No."

"Both gone?"

"That's correct."

Well, she couldn't say she was surprised. It seemed hard to picture that he'd ever even had a father or a mother. With his huge, hard, smooth chest and his infomercial abs, his deadpan expression and his lightning-bolt tattoos, Hauk FitzWyborn seemed someone not quite mortal—someone who had never been something so vulnerable as a little boy with parents who loved him. He seemed more like a creature sprung from the Norse myths, like Odin, Vili and Ve, brought into being out of ice.

"Um, your father? Tell me about him."

He gave her the lifted-eyebrow routine.

She tried again. "What was your father like, Hauk?"

"I told you. My father is dead." He'd finished his sandwich. He stood, carried his plate and empty glass to the sink, rinsed them both and put them in the dishwasher.

She refused to give up. "I'm sorry, Hauk—that he's gone. Do you…miss him?"

He reached for the towel, dried those big hands. "He's been dead for almost a decade."

"But do you miss him?"

He hung the towel on its little hook beneath the cabinets. "You behave like an American." He made it sound like some crushing insult.

She sat up straighter in her chair. "I *am* an American."

His sculpted mouth curved. Too bad it was more a sneer than a smile. "In Gullandria, the lowliest of the low will know which questions should never be asked. In Gullandria, we do not presume to ask after the dead loved ones of people we hardly know."

Wow. Two whole sentences. The man was a chatterbox, no doubt about it. And he also had a truckload and a half of nerve, to imply that *she* was presumptuous, when he wouldn't let her make a call without listening in on her speakerphone.

She kept after him. "So. You're sensitive on the subject of your father. Why is that?"

He stood there by the sink, big and broad and silent, looking at her. But she was becoming accustomed to his eagle-eyed stare. She stared right back. And she waited.

At last, he shrugged. "My father was a Wyborn. My mother was not."

She was getting the picture. "They weren't married when you were born?"

"That's right. They were never married. I am a *fitz*. For future reference, during your stay in Gullandria, when you hear that a man's name begins with *Fitz,* you will know that man is a bastard. You might think twice before asking after his family.''

"Thank you.'' She gave him the most regal of nods. ''I'll remember that.''

"The prefix *Fitz,*'' he informed her in scholarly tones, ''is one known to many lands. A child of King Henry the Eighth comes to mind. You've heard of Henry the Eighth, second of the Tudor kings of England?''

"Yes, Hauk,'' she said dryly. ''Even rude Americans take history in school.''

"A barmaid gave King Henry a son. The barmaid named the child for his father. Henry FitzRoy. The literal translation of *Fitz* is son of. Thus, Henry, son of—''

"—the king,'' she finished for him. Her mother had told her many things about her homeland. But not this painful little detail. ''Is there some reason, now, in the twenty-first century, to…label a person that way?''

"In Gullandria, we treasure the family. Life can be hard and short—not so much in recent decades, since we discovered we are rich in oil and have a valuable commodity to trade for the comforts of the modern world. But it was not always so.

"Over the generations, we have learned to count on one another. Loyalty and honor always come first. Marriage is a sacred trust. Once his wife has given him children, a man cannot divorce. With so much value on the family, it is seen as an offense against the continued survival of our people to bring children into the world without the sacrament of marriage. Certain doors are always closed to bastard children."

"But why? It's not the child's fault that his parents weren't married."

"It's nothing to do with who is at fault. There's an old saying. *Don't bicker over blame while the house burns.*" He came toward her. "You have finished your meal?"

She stared up at him, feeling, for the first time, a certain softening toward him. "What doors are closed to you, Hauk?"

He asked again, "Have you finished?"

She looked down at the bit of uneaten sandwich. "Sure, I'm finished. With lunch."

He took her plate and her glass to the sink, dumped the crust in and ran the disposal. Then he rinsed her dishes and put them in the dishwasher with his.

"Hauk?"

He turned to her and folded his huge arms over his chest. The early-afternoon sun slanting in the window made his hair shine as though it were spun from real gold.

"What doors are closed to you?"

Now, instead of staring her down, he seemed to be studying her. She knew a certain feeling of warmth inside as she saw that she had found it, the key to having an actual conversation with him. If they spoke of Gullandria, if he thought he might impart to her things she would need to know as the daughter of his king, he was willing to talk.

He asked, "Do you understand the rules of Gullandrian succession?"

"I think so." She repeated what her mother had told her long ago. "All male *jarl*—" she pronounced it *yarl,* as her mother had taught her "—and *jarl* means noble, both singular and plural—are princes, technically eligible to claim the throne when the current king dies or is no longer capable of ruling. When that happens, the jarl convene in the capital city of Lysgard and each casts a vote. The winner is the new king. The vote itself—as well as the ceremony surrounding it—is called the kingmaking."

Hauk dropped his hands to his sides. She could have sworn he almost smiled. "Very good. You have it nearly right."

"Nearly?"

"Not *all* male jarl are princes. Only all *legitimate* male jarl."

"You're saying that you, Hauk FitzWyborn, could never be king."

"That's correct. Not that I would get any real chance to be king—let alone even *want* to be king— were I legitimate in the first place. But were I not a fitz, to be chosen king would at least be a theoretical possibility."

"What about your children?"

He looked rather pleased. "Good question. As far as my children go—and still, remember, speaking theoretically—everything can be different for them."

"You mean, if you marry, then the sons your wife gives you would be eligible when the kingmaking comes around again."

"That's right—given that my wife is jarl herself."

It suddenly occurred to her that he might be married right now. That shocked her, for some reason. Nothing personal, she hurried to reassure herself silently. It wasn't about being…interested in him, as a man.

No. Of course not.

It was only that he didn't *seem* married. Just as she couldn't picture him as a vulnerable little boy with parents who took care of him, she had trouble seeing him with a wife, with children of his own.

She couldn't resist asking. "Are you? Married?"

"No. And I have no children, either. I will never have children, unless I first have a wife. That is the lesson a fitz always learns and thus, in Gullandria, bastard children are rare."

"So then," she said gently, "you'll never be king. But your children might."

"They might. But again, it's not likely. Families hold tight to ground they have gained. The sons of kings tend to become kings. They are groomed from birth with the throne in mind. Your brother, Prince Valbrand…" Hauk paused, fisted a hand at his heart and briefly bowed his head in what was clearly a gesture of respect for someone greatly valued and tragically lost. "Your brother was born to rule. He was wise beyond his years, a good and fair man. Gullandria would have prospered under him as she has thrived under His Majesty, your father." Something had happened in Hauk's cool eyes. For the first time, Elli saw that he did have a heart and that he had admired—even loved—her brother.

Her own heart contracted. "He was…good? My brother?"

"Yes. A fine man. The Gullandrian people felt pride that someday he would rule. Jarl and freeman alike knew a steady confidence in the future he would make for us all."

"And my other brother, Kylan?"

Hauk shrugged. "He was a child when we lost him. Barely in his fifth year."

"But…did you ever see him? Do you remember anything about him?"

After a thoughtful pause, he said, "Young Prince Kylan was strong and well made. He had the dark hair and eyes of the Celts—as did Prince Valbrand, as does His Majesty, your father."

Strong and well made, dark hair and eyes…

It was all so sad. Both of them, her fine, strong, dark-eyed brothers, lost now, one to a fire, one to the sea the Gullandrians loved. Lost to Elli and her shattered family. Lost to the country they might have ruled and ruled well.

Hauk approached her again. She looked up at him. "So sad…"

"Yes. A great double tragedy. For your family. For our land."

His words had so exactly echoed her thoughts. She gestured at the chair across from her. "Sit down. Please." He took the chair. "Tell me more. About Gullandria."

Hauk talked for a while, quietly. He told her that the North Atlantic drift made Gullandria's seacoasts warm for that latitude. He spoke of the famous Gullandrian horses, with their flowing white manes and long, thick white coats to protect them against the northern winters.

Elli asked, "And with my brothers gone, who do you think will be the next king?"

Hauk spoke then of a man who had been her father's friend since childhood, the man second in power only to King Osrik himself: the Grand Counselor, Medwyn Greyfell. Medwyn was several years older than Osrik, and unlikely to live to succeed him. But Greyfell had a son, Eric. The younger Greyfell was the most likely choice.

"Still," he added, shaking that golden head, "none can say with certainty how the jarl will vote when the kingmaking again comes around."

They left for her mother's house at a little after six in Elli's BMW. Hauk filled the seat beside her. His knees were cramped against the dashboard and his head touched the ceiling. They'd reached a sort of understanding in the past few hours. At least they'd found something to talk about: the land where he would soon be taking her, the land that he loved.

But looking at him, sitting there in the passenger seat, she was struck all over again with that feeling of extreme unreality: Elli and her Viking bodyguard, on their way to dinner at her mother's house...

The house where Elli had grown up was three stories, Tudor in style, on a wide, curving street lined with gorgeous mature oaks and maples. As a child, Elli and her sisters had sometimes lain on the emerald slope of the front lawn and stared up at the thick canopy of leaves overhead, smiling at the blue sky beyond, watching the clouds up there, drifting by.

The driveway was on the west side. Elli drove under an arching porte cochere to a back parking area. She stopped at the farthest door of the four-car garage.

"We'll go in the back way. I have a key, if we need it."

Hauk frowned. He looked almost comical, crammed into her sporty little car, hunching those massive shoulders so that he could fit. "It would be wiser, I think, to go to the front door, to knock."

"Oh, please. I was raised here. I don't have to knock."

"But I do."

She sighed. "Listen. I don't intend to explain *everything*. If my mother hears how you broke into my apartment, how you tied me up and planned to kidnap me, how Father has set you on me as a round-the-clock guard, she'll hit the roof. So we'll let her think you're my guest, okay? I can always bring a guest home. My mother would never object to that."

"I am a stranger here. A wise stranger enters by the front door."

Elli threw up both hands. "Will you save the platitudes? You hardly entered *my* house by the front door—and if you were really so damn wise, you would have let me come here on my own, because we both know that explaining *you* is going to be almost as difficult as convincing my poor mother to accept where I intend to go."

"I have told you, my orders—"

"I know what your orders are. And *I'm* telling *you*, I'm no stranger and you're with me, so there's no reason we can't just—"

He showed her the lightning bolt in the heart of his hand. "Someone comes."

The door to the back service porch opened and her mother's housekeeper emerged.

"That's Hilda Trawlson," Elli told Hauk. "Hildy's been with us as long as I can remember. She came back with us from Gullandria." Elli rolled down the window on Hauk's side. "Hi, Hildy!"

Hilda came down the steps and up to the car. "Elli." Her dark gaze flicked once over the Viking in the passenger seat. Then she looked again at Elli. "You've brought a guest." Her voice was flat.

"Hildy, don't be a sourpuss. This is Hauk."

The housekeeper and the warrior exchanged cautious nods.

Elli could see that Hilda already suspected Hauk had not come from Cleveland. So she announced, "Hauk is here from Gullandria."

Hilda took a step back.

Elli leaned on her door and got out of the car. "We have some things to talk about with Mom." She kept a smile on her face and her tone light. The whole idea here was to make her mother—and Hilda—believe that the coming trip was completely her choice.

And it *was* her choice. They didn't need to know that choosing *not* to go wasn't an option.

Hauk took his cue from her and pushed open his own door. Swinging those powerful legs out, he planted his big boots on the concrete and unfolded himself from the passenger seat. Hildy was giving him the evil eye. He stared back, stoic as ever. Neither deigned to speak.

"Can we just go in?" Elli asked wearily.

"Certainly." Hilda turned sharply on her crepe heel and headed toward the back door. She led them across the big service porch with its terra-cotta floor and profusion of potted plants, and from there, through the wonderful old kitchen where the green marble counters gleamed and the cabinets were fronted in beveled glass and something good was cooking, down the central hall to the family room.

"Your mother will join you shortly," the housekeeper said as she ushered them into the room.

"Is she still at work?" Elli's mother owned an antique shop downtown in Old Sac.

"She came in a few minutes ago. She only went up to change. Is there anything I can get you before I go?"

"Oh, Hildy. Will you stop it? Don't I even get a hug?"

Hildy's stern face softened slightly. "Come on, then." She held out those long arms. Elli went into them, pressing herself close to Hildy's considerable bosom, breathing in the housekeeper's familiar scent of Ivory soap and lavender, thinking that those smells, for all her life, would remind her of home.

"Everything's fine, honestly," Elli whispered to the woman who was like a dear aunt or a grandmother to her.

Hildy said nothing, just gave her an extra squeeze

before letting her go. "I'm in the kitchen, if you need me."

"I think what I *need* is a drink," Elli muttered as soon as Hildy had left them. "And don't give me that look."

Gold brows drew together over that bladelike nose. "Look?"

"Yes. There. That one." She turned for the wet bar on the inner wall. "It's almost like all your other looks, since pretty much your expression doesn't change. But there are…minute shifts. The one I just saw was the disapproving one." She found a half-full bottle of pinot grigio in the fridge and held it up. "You?"

"No."

"Now, why did I sense that was what you would say?"

"You are distressed."

She turned to look for a wineglass. "Yep. *Distressed* is the word. This is not my idea of a real fun time, you know? My mother is not going to be happy about our news. And I wish she had told me that my father had called, that he'd asked for my sisters and me. And I…" She let her voice trail off and shook her head. "You're right. Wine is tempting, but overall, a bad idea." She put the bottle away and then lingered, bent at the waist, one hand draped over the door to the half fridge, staring down into the contents. "Hmm. Diet 7UP, Mug root beer. Evian. But the question is, where are my—"

"Your Clearly Canadians are in the back, second shelf." It was her mother's voice, smooth as silk, cool as a perfectly chilled martini. She was standing in the open doorway to the hall.

"Hi, Mom." Elli flashed her mother what she hoped was an easy smile. "Hauk? What can I get you?"

"Nothing. Thank you."

Elli pulled out the tall pink bottle, shut the refrigerator and stood, her smile intact. Her mother, tall, blond as her daughters and stunningly beautiful in a crisp white shirt, a heavy turquoise necklace and black slacks, did not smile back.

"Mom, we were just—"

Ingrid wasn't listening. "Who is this man?"

What to do? How to handle this? There was just no right approach to take.

Elli gestured with her bottle of fruit-flavored sparkling water. "This is Hauk FitzWyborn."

Hauk whipped his big fist to his chest and lowered his head. "Your Majesty."

There was an awful moment of total silence.

Then her mother said, too softly, "Hildy was waiting for me at the foot of the stairs. She told me. But I refused to believe it." Ingrid was looking at Elli again, blue eyes gleaming dangerously. "Let me guess. A warrior, right? One of Osrik's goons, his…Viking berserkers?"

"Mom." Elli set the unopened bottle on the bar and went to her mother. "Come on." She took Ingrid's elbow. "Let's not—"

"Don't." Ingrid jerked free. "I want to know what's happening here. I want to know why you've brought one of your father's thugs into my house."

Chapter Six

So much for the faint hope of giving this explosive subject the delicate introduction it deserved.

Elli made it short and simple. "Hauk is here to escort me to Gullandria. I'm leaving sometime in the next two days. Father has—" What to call it? "—invited me. And I've said I will come."

Ingrid's mouth had dropped open. "I don't... You're not... Surely, you can't—"

Elli reached for her mother's arm again. "Oh, Mom. Here. Sit down." She made a shooing motion at Hauk, who still loomed nearby, hand to chest, head down, blocking the nearest chair.

Hauk got the message. He moved to the other end of the big room and pretended to stare out a window, giving them as much privacy as he could without actually leaving them alone together and going against the orders of his king.

Elli eased her mother down onto the cushions. "Mom. Please." She knelt, took Ingrid's trembling hand. "It's not the end of the world. It's…something you had to expect might happen someday, that one of us would want to go there, to meet our father face-to-face."

Ingrid was shaking her head. "No. I never in a thousand years expected that. I'd always believed I made it clear to the three of you. To go back there is a bad idea. A very, very bad idea."

Elli squeezed her mother's hand. "He *is* my father."

Ingrid leaned close. "He gave you up." She spoke low, with a terrible intensity. "Gave you up as I gave up our sons. And look what happened to them, to my little boys." It hurt to see it, the way heartache could twist such a beautiful face. She gripped Elli's hand more tightly. "Isn't it enough that both of them are dead? He has no right, *none,* to summon you now."

"But I *want* to go."

"You don't know what you're saying."

"Yes, I do. It's important to me, to know my own father, to find out for myself what he's like."

"I can't believe he's done this. I told him no. I told him absolutely not, under any circumstances." Ingrid didn't seem to realize what she'd just let slip.

Elli prompted, though she already knew the truth, "You're saying you spoke to him recently?"

Ingrid blinked. And then confessed, "Yes. He called last Friday."

"You didn't say a word to me. You didn't tell me—"

"Of course I didn't tell you." Ingrid wrapped her other hand around their joined ones. "There was no need to tell you. He called and he asked me to send you—all three of you. When I refused, he started giving orders. When giving orders didn't work, he offered me a bribe."

Elli stiffened. Her father hadn't mentioned any bribes. "You're not serious. He wouldn't—"

"Oh, yes, he would." Ingrid was nodding, her mouth a thin line. "He mentioned a figure. A large one." She added, more to herself than to Elli, "As if I need his money, as if money means a thing to me when measured against my babies."

Elli supposed, now that she thought about it, that she could see her father trying just about anything to get her mother to let him see his remaining children. "He's got to be desperate. And so very lonely now. He's lost two sons."

Ingrid made a feral sound deep in her throat. "*He's* lost two sons! It's *my* loss, too. *Our* loss, all of ours. Yours and mine and Brit's and Liv's. My sons, your brothers. Gone. Dead. And no one will ever convince me they died purely by accident. A fire in the stables and a five-year-old loses his life horribly, his poor little body burned almost beyond recognition. Wasn't that enough? Evidently not. Because now there's been a storm at sea—Valbrand washed overboard, survivors reporting they saw him swept away.

"No. There's more than misfortune at work here. In Gullandria, the rules of succession make life much too hazardous for the sons of the king. The jarl are forever forming their alliances, plotting and planning. Deep in my heart, I'll always suspect that your brothers didn't die purely by accident.''

Shock had Elli staring. ''You've never said anything like that before.''

''Of course I haven't. I've always prayed I'd never have to.''

Elli found she was determined, now, to speak with her father, to learn all that he knew about the circumstances surrounding her brothers' deaths.

Ingrid stared into the middle distance. ''I kept my word to your father. One son dead all those years ago. And then, last summer, the other vanishes. Sometimes it was like a knife, buried deep, turning cruelly inside of me, but I did what I had to do. I stayed here, in America, with you girls. I couldn't save what was gone, but I kept my promise to your father. And I kept you three safe.'' She shifted her burning gaze to Elli. ''Please. I am begging you. Don't go there. I'm afraid for you to go there.''

Elli realized her father had been right to fear she might be swayed by a visit to her mother. Ingrid was very convincing. Her arguments not only made sense, they plucked hard and hurtfully at Elli's heartstrings. Elli loved her mother. Greatly. The last thing she wanted was to see Ingrid suffer and know she herself was the cause of it.

Over by the window, Hauk turned—just enough to meet Elli's eyes. Something flashed between them: an insight, a *knowing*. Elli saw that the warrior understood exactly what she was feeling, that he had been warned by his king to expect it. It was why he guarded her so closely, why she had not been allowed to come here, to her mother, on her own.

Elli pushed her doubts aside. She had made an agreement with her father. And she would keep it.

Mustering her arguments, she spoke to Ingrid again. "It's only a visit. Three weeks. And you just said it yourself. If there is *any* danger, it's to the *sons* of a king." A king's daughter might be the only female jarl to claim the title of princess, but that didn't make her eligible for the throne. "A princess is never even considered when the *jarl* gather for the king-making."

"First time for everything," Ingrid said bleakly.

"It's not going to happen. You know it's not. And we've had no proof that Kylan and Valbrand were victims of foul play. Even the scandal sheets never hinted at anything like that."

"That doesn't mean it isn't possible."

"Mom, please look at this logically. There's no way I can be in any danger, because I am a threat to no one. I'm a kindergarten teacher from Sacramento and I'm going for a visit, that's all. In three weeks, I'll be back home where I belong."

Ingrid made a scoffing sound. "You aren't listening. You haven't heard a thing I've said."

"Yes, I *am* listening. I do understand."

"Elli, he gave me his *word,* all those years ago. He kept my sons to bring up as kings. And I got you girls. It was a vow, between us—that neither would ever try to reclaim what was lost. And you know how highly a Gullandrian holds his vow. But what's happening now?'' Her voice gained power—and volume. ''Our sons are dead. And he wants his daughters. His vow is nothing. He's a liar and a cheat.''

Elli could see Hauk. He stood very still, in profile to them, presumably looking out over the side yard. He had heard every word, of course. And he revered her father. Elli had the sense that if anyone else but his king's runaway queen had dared to utter such slanders against the ruler he served, Hauk would have been on them and it would not have been pretty.

Her mother had more to say. ''Osrik and his Grand Counselor, Greyfell, have been plotting. I know it. I can feel it in my bones. Something more than a father-and-daughter reunion is up here. Something political. Something to do with who will end up on the throne. And you are the pawn at the heart of his game. That's why he wants you, why he's taking you away.''

''It's a *visit,* Mom. Nobody said anything about taking me away.'' Well, actually, they *had.* Hauk, after all, had started out to kidnap her. But no way Elli was going into that part of the story—especially not now, with her mother looking so desperate and wild-eyed.

Ingrid let out a cry. ''Oh, my God. What about Brit and Liv? Is he after them, too?''

''No. Absolutely not. He hasn't contacted them.''

Ingrid glared down at her. ''How do you know?''

''He told me so.''

Her mother made that scoffing sound again. ''And you *believe* him?''

''Yes. I do.''

''Then you are stone-blind.'' Ingrid gestured at the

phone on the side table a few feet away. "Give me that."

"Mom—"

"Give me the phone."

With a long sigh, Elli rose and got the phone and handed it to her mother.

Ingrid punched a number from autodial and pressed the phone to her ear. After a minute, she demanded, "Liv? Is that you?" She put her hand over the mouthpiece. "Well. At least she answered." She spoke to Liv again. "Yes... No... I just... Oh, Livvy, Elli's here. Your father has contacted her.... Yes. That's right. That's what I said.... He wants her to visit him in Gullandria. She tells me she's going. She's got some big Gullandrian savage with her.... Yes, yes. Insane... You're so right. And I need to know. Have you heard from him? Has he summoned you, too?" Ingrid let out a relieved-sounding breath. "Thank God for that, at least." Ingrid cast a sharp glance at Elli, then said to Liv, "Yes. I told you. She's right here... All right." She held out the phone. "Talk to your sister. Maybe she can make you see reason."

Elli took the phone. She tried a light approach. "Hey, there. How's torts?" Liv was a law student at Stanford.

She was also ever the "big" sister, at fifty-nine minutes Elli's senior. She started right in with a lecture. "Ell, are you crazy? There is no way you can do this."

"Liv—"

"In the first place, you'll break Mom's heart if you go. And why would you even *want* to go, to take off out of nowhere for that throwback misogynistic block of ice in the Norwegian Sea? Step back. Get a grip on yourself. Ask yourself what's really happening here. Who's to say what that long-lost father of ours has in store for you once he gets you there and under his control?''

"Liv—"

"I don't like this. It scares me. It—"

"Liv."

"I don't—"

"Liv!"

There was a silence, a hostile one. Then Liv finally grumbled, "What?"

"I've talked to Father. And I've made up my mind. I *want* to do this. I *want* to meet him." She sent a glance at her mother, who stared back at her through anguished eyes. "Mom is going to accept this, eventually." Passionately, her mother shook her head. Elli said slowly and clearly, "I don't believe for a minute that Father would ever do me—or any of us—harm. I'm going to be fine. I'll be back in three weeks and I want you *not* to worry."

Liv swore under her breath. "You're so easy most of the time. It was always Brit and I fighting over who got to run things. You'd just go along. But every once in a while, you'd decide to take a stand for your own way. And whenever you did..."

"That's right. You two couldn't budge me. One time in a hundred, we'd do what I wanted. And this is that one time."

"It *is* strange, you have to admit it. He doesn't

know any of us. He's made no *effort* to know us. Why now—and why did he pick on you in particular?"

"Why now? I think it's obvious. With Valbrand gone, he can't help but think of the daughters he's never known."

"Then why you?"

"I don't know. But I intend to find out, I promise you that."

"If anything happens to you in that place, I swear I will kill you."

Elli couldn't help smiling. "I love you, Livvy. I'll be fine."

"You'd better keep in touch on this."

"You know I will."

Ingrid took the phone again to say goodbye. The minute she disconnected the call, she tried Brit's apartment in L.A. Brit's machine answered. Ingrid left a message. After that, she dialed Brit's cell, and then her *other* cell—Brit was forever losing her cell phones.

Increasingly frantic, Ingrid tried the numbers she had for three of Brit's friends. The third one finally picked up the phone. She suggested Ingrid try to reach Brit at work.

Brit was a licensed pilot. She'd eaten beetles and jumped from a skyscraper on *Fear Factor*. She'd trekked the Amazon and the New Zealand wilderness. She'd also dropped out of college after only two years. Like Elli and Liv, Brit had a hefty regular income from a well-managed trust, but Brit was forever giving her money away and inevitably ran short before the next check came in.

So she worked. At a series of menial jobs.

Currently, she was waiting tables at an Italian restaurant on East Melrose, where the owner was Greek and all the cooks were from south of the border. Everybody hated to call her there. The owner did a lot of shouting whenever Brit used the phone.

But Ingrid was desperate. She dialed the number—and sighed in relief when Brit came on the line.

Ingrid asked her youngest daughter the same questions she'd asked Liv. She got the same answers. Brit was fine, too. No sign of any Vikings in her life. And she wanted to talk to Elli.

So Elli took the phone and explained what she'd already explained to Liv, while in the background, the owner of the restaurant yelled at Brit to get to work and Brit had to pause every couple of minutes to shout at him to get off her back.

"Just stay in touch, okay?" Brit demanded, echoing Liv.

"I will. I love you. Don't work too hard."

"Hah. Like I've got a choice in this place. It's a hellhole, I'm telling you."

The call to Brit seemed to get Ingrid more upset than before. But Ingrid always got upset when it came to her underemployed, fearless, free-spirited youngest daughter.

Elli tried again to soothe her mother, promising over and over that she'd be all right, she'd keep in touch.

Hilda finally called them to dinner. They sat at the big table in the formal dining room—and Ingrid turned her fear and fury on Hauk.

"What is going on between you and this man, Elli? Why did you bring him here? He watches you—" she gave a frantic laugh "—like a hawk." The laughter died in her throat and she glared at Hauk. "You behave like a bodyguard. Is there some reason my daughter needs a bodyguard?"

Elli spoke up. "Of course I don't need a bodyguard, Mother. I told you why Hauk is here. He'll escort me to Gullandria. I invited him to dinner because it seemed the polite thing to do." Yes, it was an outright lie. But what help would the truth be at this point? In the end, in spite of her mother's endless and convincing arguments, Elli intended to keep her word and go to her father.

She said softly, "I realize now it was probably... unwise to bring him to dinner. I'm sorry."

Hauk let Elli's answer stand for him. He was not a stupid man. He must have understood that anything he said would only make matters worse.

In the end, Ingrid seemed to realize that nothing she could do would stop Elli from going to Gullandria. She agreed to care for the cats and extracted a promise from Elli that she would call as soon as she reached her father's palace.

At a little after nine, Ingrid stood in the driveway, waving, a brave smile on her lips, as Elli and Hauk drove away.

"I think you should pack now," Hauk announced right after Elli unlocked her apartment door and let them both inside.

Elli didn't want to pack. She didn't want to do

anything right then, except maybe sit on the couch in the dark and watch something mindless on TV and pretend that she hadn't told all those lies to her mother, pretend that she hadn't heard all the troubling things her mother had said about her father and her brothers and the land where her father lived.

Hauk stood before her, huge and unmoving and waiting for her answer.

"You think I should pack, huh?" she asked provokingly.

"I do."

"Well, what you think is your business. I'm not packing now." She dropped her purse and keys on the table.

Hauk said, "The royal jet is ready and waiting, with the crew on call, at Sacramento Executive Airport. If you pack, we can leave tonight. The Gulfstream has its own bedroom suite. You will be comfortable. You can sleep in flight."

Elli had wandered into the living room and picked up the remote. She tossed it back down again. "I was just thinking that what I'd like to do more than anything right now is watch TV and forget everything that's happened around here since you showed up yesterday and turned my whole life upside down. But just this moment, I realized, that if I watch TV, I won't be able to forget anything. Because you'll be here, sitting in that chair, watching me, guarding me against the possibility that I might do something *I* want to do rather than what my father wants. I have to tell you, Hauk, I find that upsetting. You could say that it really ticks me off."

"You should pack. We should leave."

"I'm not packing now. I'm not *leaving* now. And you have nothing at all to say about that, because it's not Thursday and I have until Thursday if I *want* until Thursday."

"There is no need to linger here."

"Not to you, maybe."

"Other than to pack, you're ready to go now."

"You're not getting it. I may be ready, but I'm not *ready.*" She turned for the hall, then paused and turned back to him. "I'm taking a bath. This time, I'm staying in there awhile because it's the only place I can go right now where you *won't* be."

He had that soldier-at-attention look he liked to get when he wasn't quite sure what she was going to do next—let alone how he ought to *handle* what she was going to do next.

She glared at him. "I want an hour. To myself. Is that understood?"

"Yes."

She went to her room and from there to her bathroom and the second she got in there, she shut the door. Hard.

Sixty minutes later—she had a travel clock she kept on the bathroom shelf, so she was able to time herself—she emerged from the bathroom. Hauk was waiting, boots off and bedroll at the ready, by the foot of her bed.

She considered heading into the living room to channel surf in the dark for a while as she had threatened to do earlier. But he'd only follow her. Might as well channel surf from the comfort of her bed.

She climbed under the covers and the cats came and cuddled in with her. Hauk continued to stand, staring off toward the door.

"Is there some problem?" she demanded sourly. He wasn't in the way of the TV, but he was distracting in the extreme, just standing there. It was like having a giant statue at the foot of her bed.

The statue spoke. "You are upset about the visit with your mother and that has put you in a contrary frame of mind. It's possible you will rethink your decision to go to bed at this time. I see no reason to become comfortable if you're only going to go elsewhere."

"Comfortable? What are you talking about? You never become comfortable. You never even *sleep*."

"I sleep. Perhaps not as you would perceive sleep to be. I am capable of maintaining a state of readiness while technically sleeping."

"A state of readiness."

"Yes."

She resisted the urge to hurl the remote at him. "Hauk."

"Yes?"

"Lie down."

He dropped to his blankets, disappearing from her view.

She petted her cats, watched back-to-back *Buffy* reruns and told herself she was ignoring him. A state of readiness. Oh, *fershure*.

At eleven, she turned off the television and rolled

on her side. By midnight, she couldn't stand it. She sat up and turned on the lamp and grabbed the phone.

"Who are you calling?" His voice came from the foot of the bed. She couldn't see him. He hadn't even sat up.

"My mother. And I'm not putting it on speakerphone, so don't you dare try to make me." She clutched the phone tightly, ready to whack him with it if he rose up from below the footboard.

She thought she heard him sigh. "All right. Keep your word. Say nothing to endanger your visit to your father."

"I hate you, Hauk."

"Make your call."

Her mother answered on the first ring. "Elli?"

"I love you, Mom. I'll be fine. Please don't worry."

There was a silence, then Ingrid said, "I won't." They both knew it was a lie, but a *good* lie, a loving mother's lie. "Thank you, darling. For calling. I've been lying here thinking of you."

"I know. I was thinking of you, too."

A low, sad little chuckle came over the line. "Isn't it ironic? Liv is so headstrong. And Brit? Well, we all know Brit is the type of daughter to make her mother prematurely gray. But you? An excellent student, always so reasonable. You were the one I went to when I needed help convincing one of your sisters not to do something dangerous or harebrained."

"Mom…"

"Oh, I know, I know. This is something you feel you have to do. And it's your choice to make."

"That's right."

"Hilda will be over tomorrow to pick up Diablo and Doodles."

"That should work."

"Elli."

"What, Mom?"

"Have a good trip. A *safe* trip."

"I will, Mom. I'll be back before you know it and…our lives will go on."

"Good night my own sweet Little Old Giant."

Elli whispered, "Good night, Mom," and hung up the phone.

From the end of the bed, there was silence.

"Hauk?"

"Yes?"

"I don't really hate you."

"I know."

Elli turned off the light and rolled onto her side. Within a few minutes, she was asleep.

Hauk lay awake.

Wide-awake.

As a rule, he possessed considerable discipline when it came to the time for sleep. He'd been trained and trained well. Sleep, like good nourishment and regular physical exercise to muscular exhaustion and beyond, was a main building block of superior performance. He could sleep in a snow cave, in subzero temperatures with enemies on every side—and be ready to snap wide-awake at the smallest strange movement or sound. As he'd told Elli—

He caught his own dangerous thoughts up short. Not simply Elli. Never simply Elli.

She was the princess. Her Highness. *Princess* Elli. But never her name by itself.

From thought sprang action. And he couldn't allow his thoughts to become too familiar. It was unacceptable. More than unacceptable.

It was forbidden.

He wanted her on that plane. He wanted her safe with his liege and out of his hands.

But she *would* balk, would stall—would keep insisting she had until Thursday and she wasn't leaving until then. The more he tried to get her to go, the more determined she became to stay.

Dangerous, the games she played. For more reasons than she allowed herself to understand. Not only was *she* stuck with *him,* every moment, as she never seemed to tire of reminding him; *he* was stuck with *her.* He could go nowhere, do nothing, without keeping her in sight.

This was the kind of assignment that, under most circumstances, he could do with one eye closed and a hand tied behind his back. Second nature. To watch. To guard. To remain detached and yet vigilant. Over the years, he'd delivered a number of important personages—and dangerous prisoners—into the proper hands.

But this, he was learning, was *not* most circumstances. This was the daughter of his king. And something was happening to him, in this period of forced proximity with her. Something that had never happened to him before.

He let himself think it: *She draws me. I* want *her....*

He could hardly believe it. He'd thought himself well beyond such ridiculous weakness. A warrior, in particular the king's warrior, learned early to effectively sublimate physical needs—especially sexual ones, which were no use at all to a soldier in his work.

And yet, in a mere twenty-four hours, it had happened. This troublesome princess had somehow managed, all unknowing, to get under his skin.

He found himself doing things he despised. Noticing the fresh, flowerlike scent of her. More than noticing. May the three Norns of destiny curse him, he was constantly sniffing the air when she was near. And he watched her. All the time. Yes, it was his duty to watch her. But he was not supposed to take such pleasure in the task.

It was hopeless, this growing hunger he felt for her. Counterproductive in the extreme. The woman was so completely beyond his touch. So far above him that his king had not even bothered to remind him to keep his hands off.

Hauk didn't know for certain what scheme his king was hatching, but he knew that Queen Ingrid was right. His lord had plans for Princess Elli. And those plans did not include her lying down with her father's bastard warrior. It would be a huge and unpardonable betrayal of honor and his king's trust for Hauk to lay a hand on her, except as required in the furtherance of his duty.

Still—in spite of how wrong it was, no matter the complete lack of discipline it showed—the woman enchanted him. She wove a spell over him, with her huge eyes and soft mouth, her clever tongue and quick mind. And her heart.

Yes, that was surely her most alluring feature. That seeming contradiction of softness and strength only found in a woman with a true and loving heart. She would be a prize beyond price to the man who claimed her.

And he would never be that man.

Yet his orders forced him to this—to spending the nights at the foot of her bed—scenting her, listening to her small, sweet sighs as she dreamed.

It was the purest kind of torture. A taste of Valhalla. A visit to Hel.

And there was no way to make an end to it until she gave up and agreed to go—or until Thursday came at last.

Chapter Seven

When Elli woke in the morning, Hauk was gone from his place at the foot of her bed.

But this time she had no illusions that he might have given up and returned to Gullandria without her. She tossed back the covers and went into the bathroom to wash her face and get dressed. When she got back to the bedroom, there he was, dressed in a fresh black shirt and black slacks, his square jaw smooth from a recent shave.

Waiting.

Elli sighed. "Let's get some breakfast."

"As you wish."

Over scrambled eggs and toast, he suggested again that she pack so that they could leave.

Elli just looked at him, a long look. She knew a

bleak satisfaction when he was the first to glance away.

Hilda came knocking at a little before noon. She scowled when she saw that Elli had a houseguest.

"Why is he here? He doesn't need to be here."

Elli finessed an answer. "I told you, he's my escort. We're leaving together tomorrow."

Hilda never stopped scowling the whole time she was there. Elli put the cats in their carrier and Hauk helped her haul all the cat supplies down to Hilda's 4×4.

"Do I get a goodbye hug?" Elli asked the housekeeper just before she drove away.

Hilda relented enough to bestow the hug, but kept her scowl in place. And of course, about fifteen minutes after she and the cats departed, Ingrid called.

"You didn't tell me that thug was staying at your apartment."

"Oh, Mom. It's no big deal. I have a spare room." Too bad Hauk refused to sleep in it unless she did.

"Still, he has no right to—"

"Mom. Let it be. Please."

A silence echoed down the line. Then her mother murmured, "Yes. I suppose you're right." She wished Elli well again and reminded her to call.

"I will. I promise."

They said goodbye. Elli hung up.

Hauk was right there, maybe three feet away. Watching. Listening.

Elli decided she might possibly go insane if she had to stay cooped up in her apartment all day with two hundred-plus pounds of Viking observing her every move. She reached for her purse. "Come on."

He frowned at her. "You wish to leave now?"

"That's right."

"You have yet to pack your belongings."

"You are so very, very observant."

He might have flinched at that one. But if so, it was a tiny flinch—so small it probably hadn't really happened at all. "You don't wish to take anything with you?"

"To Gullandria?"

"Yes. To Gullandria."

"Well, as a matter of fact, I do intend to take a few things to Gullandria."

"Then hadn't you better pack them?"

"Not now."

He looked at her steadily, his expression especially bleak. He knew by then that she was up to something.

And she was. "We're not going to Gullandria. Not yet, anyway." She waited. She wanted him to ask, *Then where are we going?* But apparently, he'd decided not to give her the satisfaction. Fine. She told him anyway. "We're going to a movie."

"A movie. Why?"

"Because it's Wednesday. Because I *can.*"

She took him to the latest James Bond thriller. Who could say? Maybe he'd be able to relate. At the snack counter, she bought a jumbo tub of popcorn drizzled with butter flavoring and a large Sprite.

"We can share the popcorn," she told him. "Want a Coke or something?"

"No, thank you."

She accepted her Sprite from the guy behind the counter, who kept shooting sideways glances at Hauk. Elli supposed she wasn't surprised. Hauk was hardly your average Joe. He stood at least a head taller than anyone else in the sparse weekday-afternoon crowd around them. And then there were all those muscles, that proud military bearing—not to mention the shoulder-length golden hair. Even with his shirt on, so you couldn't see the blue-and-gold lightning bolt that blazed across his chest, Hauk could have walked right off a martial arts movie poster.

Elli realized she might actually be starting to enjoy herself a little. She grinned. Oh, yes. *Enter the Viking.* Or maybe *Warriors of the North.*

"You're smiling. Why?" Hauk's voice was low. Somehow, it sounded right next door to intimate.

Elli felt a shiver run beneath her skin. How odd. "Oh, nothing. Here." She shoved the tub of popcorn at him. He took it and she got herself a straw and a handful of napkins and led the way up the ramp to the little stand where the ticket taker waited.

There were thirteen theaters in the building. Each of them had Dolby sound and big, comfortable seats, like easy chairs, well padded with high backs and plenty of room between the rows. Still, in deference to Hauk's massive frame, Elli chose the row in back, which had an extra-wide aisle between it and the next row down.

Once they were seated in the dark, he offered her the popcorn tub. "Oh, you go ahead and hold it," she said.

"I don't care for any."

She started to take it from him. And then a naughty whim took her. "Hold it anyway—because I am your princess, right? Because, after my father, you serve me."

He looked at her for a long time, his eyes shining at her through the darkness. "That's right. I serve you."

A small tremor went through her, a quivery feeling. Her heart beat too fast and her cheeks felt warm.

Was something happening here?

Oh, of course not.

The dark screen lit up and the preshow snack-bar advertisements of dancing paper cups and singing candy boxes began.

The movie was your usual James Bond flick. Fast-paced, fun to watch, with lots of drop-dead-gorgeous women and Pierce Brosnan, the perfect James Bond, dark and sleek, killer handsome, delightfully urbane.

Elli sipped her Sprite and intermittently munched her popcorn and wished her silly heart would stop pounding so fast every time she reached over and grabbed a handful out of Hauk's lap.

Okay, she'd blundered. She should have taken the tub when he tried to give it back to her. She should have thought about how awkward it was going to be, how…intimate, to keep groping for fistfuls of popcorn while he was holding the container.

Intimate.

It was the second time that particular word had come to mind since they'd entered the theater complex.

But what was so strange about that?

Not a thing. Not considering the way it was between them, the way she had to be with him virtually round-the-clock. Even though they weren't *really* intimate, it was hard not to think of the word. Intimate, at least in part, meant to be physically close. And *that* they were.

Oh, yes, they were.

She could feel the heat coming off his big body. And the outer side of her upper arm touched his, just barely, all the time. And then there was the scent of him, that scent of cedar and spice and...maleness. That scent that she did find so dangerously attractive.

He whispered, out of the side of his mouth, "You're not eating your popcorn." She could have sworn she heard humor in his voice.

Humor.

And intimacy.

She looked at him sharply. He was staring at the screen.

And wasn't that the main reason she'd dragged him here? To give him something else to stare at but her.

She hadn't thought it through, though. Hadn't considered that they'd be sitting so close their bodies brushed, that she'd have the bad judgment to make a big deal of ordering him to hold the popcorn for her.

She whispered, "Um, are you sure you don't want any popcorn?"

"Yes. I'm sure."

"Then I guess I'll just hold it myself."

He leaned a fraction nearer, heat and size and maleness pressing in. "Are you certain? I am willing to serve." His voice was low and soft and…silky.

Elli's mouth went bone-dry. She gulped. "I…yeah. I'm certain."

He handed her the tub, the pads of his big fingers brushing hers. A bullet of heat went shooting through her, so thrilling it was painful—from where his fingers grazed hers, straight up her arm—and right to her chest, which contracted sharply, so that she almost gasped.

They were staring at each other. The Dolby sound swelled around them and images flashed on the big screen, reflecting at them, so that Hauk's chiseled profile gleamed alabaster in the darkness. His hair shone, not gold, not platinum, but some rare color in between.

He was the one who looked away, back at the screen. And this time she felt no triumph that he did. This time, she felt it as a tearing sensation, that he ripped something, left tattered raw edges, when he looked away.

She stared at him for several bewildered seconds, thinking what she shouldn't be thinking: that he was so very wonderfully male. That it would be a lovely, thrilling thing to have his big hands on her, to press her mouth to his…

When they came out of the movie, it was a little after three. Hauk pushed the glass door open for her and she walked out, across the covered ticket booth area and into the bright sunlight of a beautiful afternoon. Overhead, the sky was clear and powder-blue.

And she wasn't ready—not yet—to go back to her place and be cooped up in there with Hauk. She headed for Land Park.

Hauk saw they weren't going where he'd assumed they'd be going. "Where are we going now?"

"To Land Park."

"You wish to see your mother again?"

"No. Not to my mother's house. Just into the park. I want to walk by the duck pond." She added, turning to give him a sarcastic smile, "Is that all right with you?"

Their gazes collided. A shimmer of heat went through her. "Return to your apartment," he said softly. "Pack your belongings. I'll take you to the plane."

Elli yanked her gaze back to the street in front of her. She had to be careful. She could get them in an accident. "No. Not yet."

"This is foolish."

And it was. She knew it. Something more than a James Bond flick had happened in the darkened movie theater. They'd emerged into the sunshine with everything changed between them—or if not changed, at least mutually acknowledged.

Looking back, it seemed that maybe there had been attraction between them almost from the very first. She'd denied it. That hadn't been difficult. What self-respecting woman would ever willingly admit that her kidnapper made her heart go pitter-pat? Not Elli.

But time had done it, made her see it. Time and the forced closeness that they shared. She was coming to know him a little, coming to understand that though she despised the job he was doing, she didn't—she *couldn't*—despise the man himself. She knew there was goodness in him. That honor and loyalty meant more to him than life. How could she help but admire that? How could she help but let down her guard with him, at least a little?

Now it seemed terribly dangerous to imagine the night to come, should she continue to insist on remaining in Sacramento until the last possible moment her agreement with her father allowed.

She should do what Hauk kept trying to get her to do. Pack. Get on that plane.

And yet, she held back. Beyond this impossible attraction to the man her father had sent to kidnap her, she had other issues here.

The more she thought about this whole situation, the more suspicious she became of her father's motives. What if her mother was right? *Could* she be walking blind into some ugly palace plot?

Her doubts ate at her. True, she *was* going. Hauk would make certain of that. But she saw no reason to rush headlong into the jaws of a possible trap.

Who knew what might happen in the next eighteen hours or so? It didn't seem particularly likely, but some new and valuable piece of information just might come to light. Maybe everything would become clear, after all.

Right, whispered a knowing voice in the back of her mind. *Everything might become clear. Oh, certainly. Anything might happen….*

Now, that did ring true. Anything might happen, all right—between her and Hauk.

Elli tossed her head. "I don't care. I don't want to go yet. I'm not sure I want to go at all."

She waited for the man beside her to tell her that she had no choice. She'd vowed to go and she *would* go.

He said nothing.

Land Park boasted its own outdoor amphitheater across from a children's amusement area called Fairytale Town and not far from the zoo. Below the amphitheater, sparkling in the afternoon sun, lay the duck pond.

Elli parked the car above the amphitheater, to the side a little. A steep, tree-shadowed, grass-covered hill swept down to the pond. They got out and Elli took off at a run down the grassy slope. Maybe she'd leave him behind.

Yeah, right.

Elli kept running anyway, not looking back, almost tumbling head-over-heels once or twice, but somehow managing to keep her feet.

Hauk followed close behind. She could *feel* him there. Never once did he stumble. And she knew he wasn't running full-out, that he effortlessly paced himself to keep a few yards back.

She reached the base of the slope, where the ground leveled out, drawing to a halt on the asphalt path that encircled the perimeter of the pond. Ducks and geese glided on the sun-sparkled surface and oaks and sweet gums grew at intervals along the bank, inviting wooden benches waiting beneath them.

Slightly breathless, she turned to Hauk. "It's pretty, isn't it?"

His sky-blue gaze darkened. "Beautiful."

She knew what he meant and it wasn't the duck pond. Her mouth was dry again. She swallowed.

He looked away from her. "What now?"

Good question. "Let's, uh, walk."

He started walking. Fast.

"Hey, wait up."

He stopped where he was. She hurried and caught up.

They stood on the path, facing each other. He was looking at her again—gazing at her as if he would eat her up. And she *liked* it, to have him look at her that way.

He said, as if it hurt him to tell her, "You *will* have to go. I will have to make you go."

"I know. But not till tomorrow. You won't make me go…until tomorrow."

"You enjoy this? Pushing the boundaries? Tempting the fates?"

Anger sizzled through her. "I'll tell you what I *don't* enjoy. Being kept in the dark. Knowing that if I break my word, you'll make me keep it anyway."

"You are jarl. High jarl. A princess."

"Did you think I'd forgotten?"

"You are a princess and a princess keeps her word."

The ducks drifted, elegant and easy, on the pond. The tree branches swayed in the slight breeze. A hundred yards away, on a swath of green across the street, a woman and a small blond child sat on a pink blanket beneath an oak, eating ice cream. The cars rolled past on the street, each one observing the speed limit. Everything seemed peaceful and perfect. Idyllic.

Except between Elli and Hauk. Between them, the air crackled. With hostility. And with heat.

She demanded with a low voice, "Do you know more of what drives my father than you're telling me?"

"No."

"If you *did* know more, *would* you tell me?"

"I can't say. It would depend."

"On?"

"What I knew. What I was ordered to keep to myself, what I thought *wise* to keep to myself."

"So, I can't really trust you, then. You could be lying to me now. You *would* lie to me now—if my father had ordered you to lie, if you thought you *should* lie."

"You knew that from the first. And you *can* trust me. To take you where you need to go, to keep you safe."

"Where *I* need to go?"

"Yes. By your own vow, I will take you where you need to go."

She was recalling the things her mother had said. "Do you think it's possible that my father hopes I might somehow claim the throne of Gullandria once he's gone?"

"No."

He had replied almost before she had the question out of her mouth. She couldn't hold back a sharp little laugh. "Well, you had no trouble answering that one."

"You think like an American."

"You said that before."

"And it remains as true now as it was then. There will be a kingmaking when your father is gone. And a prince will be chosen to succeed him. A prince. Not a princess. And certainly not a princess raised across the sea, a woman not even brought up in our ways."

She looked at him sideways. "You could use a woman ruler. You might learn a few things. You could get out of the Dark Ages and start treating women as the equals they are."

"A woman may never sit on the throne of Gullandria. But that doesn't mean a woman doesn't have rights—more rights, in some cases, than a man."

"Rights like…?" She began walking along the path.

Hauk fell in step with her. "She can own property. She is equal, as an heir, when a parent dies."

"Equal in terms of property rights. Well, good. That's something. But you said *more* rights."

"Yes. Our marriage laws give the woman the power. You'll recall I told you that a man can't divorce after his wife gives him children?"

"I remember."

"I didn't tell you that a woman *can* divorce her husband. A woman has the right to divorce at any time, simply because she believes the marriage is unworkable."

"I assume there is some reasoning behind that."

"It is thought that a woman is more responsible in

matters of hearth and home, that she would be less likely to break the vows of marriage for frivolous reasons.''

Elli hated to say it—but she did, anyway. ''I don't agree with that. I think men and women should have the *same* rights. I don't think one—either one—should have more power than the other.''

''You have plans to change our laws?''

''It was just an opinion.''

''There's an old saying. *An opinion means only as much as the power and intention of the one who owns it.*''

She arched an eyebrow at him. ''Are you implying my opinion doesn't mean much?''

She could have sworn he almost smiled. ''It's only a saying. Take what you will from it.''

Ahead of them on the path, an old man tore at a loaf of bread and tossed the pieces into the pond. The ducks gathered, nipping up the soggy bits. Bold pigeons scrambled around at his feet, gobbling the crumbs that fell to the walk from his hand.

Elli paused. ''You think maybe my father plans to marry me off to someone, then?''

Hauk paused, too, and they faced each other once more. ''It is not my place to think. Not about the intentions of my king.''

''You've said that a hundred times. But I mean, you know, go with it for a minute. What would be gained, if he married me off to some prince or other?''

Hauk lowered his head, a gesture she had come to realize was meant to display his subservience. ''I cannot play this word game with you. I have already said more than I should have.''

''Why? We're just…talking. Just sharing opinions.'' She gave him a grin. ''Minus power. And intention.''

''You have a fine mind. And a devious one.''

''Hey. I guess I'll fit in just great at my father's court.''

''I think you will—and I cannot help you scheme against my king.''

''I'm not scheming. I'm only—''

''Enough.'' He walked on. The old man saw him coming and stepped out of his path. The pigeons scattered.

Elli had to hurry to keep up.

A short time later, they went back to the apartment where Elli found two messages on her machine. One from a girlfriend and one from a guy she'd known a couple of years ago, while she was still in school at UC Davis.

Hauk stood right there as she played the messages back. He shrugged. ''Just leave them. You can answer them when you return.''

''Well, that's reassuring. You seem to think I *will* return. Too bad my own mother fears otherwise.''

He had that locked-up-tight look he got whenever he decided that responding to her would get him nowhere.

He was right to get that look. She said, ''I'll answer them now, thank you very much.''

He made her return the calls on speakerphone. He

stood there, listening to every word as she told her girlfriend she couldn't do lunch this weekend and asked for a rain check, then told the old school friend, David Saunders—in town just for a couple of days on business—that she wouldn't be able to meet him for a drink. She was leaving town tomorrow. A family trip. David said maybe next time.

"That would be great. Give me a call."

"You know I will."

She hung up and glared at Hauk. "You enjoy this? Listening in on my private conversations?"

"No."

"Then maybe you should stop doing it."

He turned away, shaking his golden head.

And that angered her.

More than angered her.

All at once, she was utterly furious with him. She grabbed his arm.

He froze.

Beneath her hand, his silky flesh felt as it if had been poured over steel. Her palm burned at the contact, her fingers flamed. The heat seemed to sizzle along her arm, blazing on, up over her shoulder and down into the center of her, making a pool of molten fire in her lower belly.

She let go, brought her hand to her mouth—and it was like touching him all over again, pressing her skin that had been on *his* skin against her lips.

She lowered her hand, slowly. Carefully. She felt shaken to the core—and ashamed of herself, too. "I...uh...sorry. Honestly. I got so angry. It was stupid. I shouldn't have grabbed you like that."

His eyes seemed to bore holes right through her. "Pack. Now."

She bit her lip, shook her head.

"You will destroy us both," he whispered.

"No. That's ridiculous. It's an...attraction, that's all. It happens between men and women. It's natural. We don't have to act on it. And if we did—which we *won't*—it would be nobody's business but yours and mine."

He was scanning her face again, his gaze burning where it touched. "You understand nothing."

Fury flared again within her. She ordered it down. "Well, then." She spoke calmly. Reasonably. "I guess you'd better explain it to me."

He didn't reply—not right away. She started to think he *wouldn't* reply. But at last, he said, "I am assigned to bring you to your father. That is all the extent of the contact you will ever have with me. Whatever your father has planned for you, I am not a part of it. I could never be a part of it, not in any way."

"My father told you that?"

"He had no need to tell me. It's fact, pure and simple. It's true that if fortune smiles on me, the daughter of some minor jarl might agree to reach out and clasp my hand in marriage. But no king would willingly give his daughter to a bastard. Some doors, as I told you, are forever closed to me."

"Not to me, Hauk. Never to me. I'm the one who decides who I'll be with, not my father. He has no rights at all when it comes to my private life."

"That may be. I am in no position to say. However,

your father does have rights over me. He has *all* rights. I live and breathe for him. All my acts are acts in his service. I am *his* warrior. It is a high honor. And a sacred trust.''

Chapter Eight

By tacit agreement, there was silence between them.

Hauk went where she went within the apartment. In the living room, she sat on the couch and he sat in the easy chair. She read—or she tried to read, though she continually lost her place and had to go back and reread whole passages to have any idea what she was reading about. She could feel his eyes on her the whole time—or so it seemed.

But then, when she couldn't stand it a moment longer and glanced up, he would be looking not *at* her, but beyond her, into the distance. His body would be so very still and straight. She would stare at his chest, wondering if he was even breathing.

Eventually, he'd draw himself back from whatever distant meditative state he'd put himself in. He'd meet her eyes.

And she'd know that he had been there all the time, watching—and yet not watching. Across the room from her. And a million miles away.

Around five, she gave up on her book and went into the spare room. She tried to pretend Hauk wasn't sitting on the futon behind her as she paid a few bills to get them out of the way and answered a few last e-mails, then put her various listserves on No-mail.

By seven or so, she was starting to get that frantic feeling—that feeling that if they remained alone in her apartment, just the two of them, for much longer, she would do something unforgivable.

Start screaming like a maniac. Start throwing things—favorite figurines, a lamp or two.

Climb him like a big tree, grab him close and kiss him, force him to put aside everything he believed in and make love with her.

Oh, how had this happened? How had this gone so dangerously far so very, very fast?

She honestly wasn't some sex maniac. Okay, she wasn't a virgin—but she was no wild thing, either.

Serious relationships? She'd had a few—well, if you included her two high-school boyfriends. One in sophomore year and one when she was a senior. At the time, she'd been certain she would love each of those boys forever and ever. But she'd grown up and so had they.

Surely this crazy attraction to Hauk was like her schoolgirl crushes—destined to flare high and hot and then, soon enough, fade away. It was the lure of the forbidden. And they'd both get over it.

Maybe he was right. She should throw some stuff

in her suitcase and tell him she was finally ready to head for Gullandria.

But somewhere deep inside, she had a true stubborn streak. She wasn't leaving until she *had* to leave and she didn't have to leave until tomorrow. She shoved the chicken she'd never gotten around to roasting into the freezer and told Hauk they were going out for dinner.

He didn't argue. He didn't say anything. He kept his sculpted mouth shut and his expression closed against her, as he'd been doing for hours by then.

She took him to a restaurant over in Old Sacramento, where the food was excellent and so was the service. The steward brought the wine list. She waved it away.

Yes, a glass of wine or two would have soothed her frayed nerves right then. But she couldn't afford to be soothed. When they went to bed tonight, she would need all her inhibitions firmly in place—and not because she feared that Hauk might make a move on her. He had way too much self-control to do that.

No, he wasn't the one she was worried about. It was herself. She would need to fight her own wayward, hungry heart and her yearning body, too, if she planned to get through the whole night without doing something they would both later regret.

Hauk spoke with the waiter briefly but politely. He *didn't* speak to Elli, not the whole time they sat at that table. Anyone watching them probably would have guessed that they'd either been forced against their will to share a meal—or they were locked in some private battle, some intimate tiff, and currently refusing to speak to each other. Both speculations would have been right on the money.

Too soon, the meal was finished. It was only 8:15. She didn't want to go back to her apartment, not yet. She wanted it to be late—after midnight at least, when they got there. She wanted to be really, really tired.

But every nerve she had was humming. She felt as if sleeping was something she would never do again. And she'd made the mistake of drinking two glasses of water with her meal.

She had to use the ladies' room.

Hauk stood outside in the hall. She hoped it embarrassed him, to lurk there by the ladies'-room door. She used the facilities and she washed her hands, glancing now and then at her unhappy face in the wide mirror above the sink.

She was blowing her hands dry when the small window over the center stall caught her eye. It was a single pane of pebbled glass, roughly a foot and a half on each side, hinged at the top. To open it, you undid the latch and pushed it outward.

She was reasonably certain there would be an alley on the other side. It wouldn't be that difficult to hoist herself up there, to slither through it and...

What? Run away? Go into hiding and terrify her mother and Hilda and her sisters, too? Go to the police? Tell them that her father was having her kidnapped and she needed protection?

After they sorted it all out, they might even believe her. And just maybe they'd be able to protect her. It was a good chance, with all the publicity that would ensue, with her face and the faces of everyone in her family splashed all over the tabloids, that her father would back off, give up on whatever scheme he was hatching.

Hauk would be disgraced for letting her get away. And she would stay right here, in Sacramento, where she belonged. She would not see Gullandria—or her father, after all. And she would never see Hauk again.

The dryer had turned itself off. The ladies' room seemed very quiet.

Behind her, the door to the hallway swung open. She turned. It was Hauk. He looked at her and he looked at the window above the center stall and then at her again.

"So all right," she muttered. "I was tempted. But notice I'm still here."

"Ahem. Do you *mind?*" A short, cute redheaded woman had appeared in the open doorway beside Hauk. She craned her neck to look up at him. "Read the sign on the door. *Ladies.* That is *so* not you."

Hauk retreated and the redhead came forward. The door closed with him out in the hall. The redhead pretended to fan herself. "Is that *yours?* Oh, my, my…"

Elli let a smile answer for her. She hooked her purse over her shoulder and went out to join her jailer.

Out in the parking lot, the attendant brought her car. She tipped him and got behind the wheel. Hauk hunched himself down into the passenger seat.

Elli drove—out of Old Sac, out of town, beyond the city lights.

More than once, she felt Hauk's brooding gaze on

her. She knew he was wondering where they were going. But he didn't ask.

Which was just as well, since she didn't know, anyway. She held the wheel and watched the road ahead and kept on driving.

They ended up on the river road, rolling through a string of sleepy little one-stoplight towns. When she was in her teens, she and her sisters and their friends—or sometimes she and one of those two boys she'd thought she loved so much—would come out here.

With a boyfriend, she'd end up parked by the levee, in the shadows of the cottonwood trees, kissing until her lips hurt, moaning and sighing and declaring undying love—all, of course, without going all the way.

Back then, Elli and her sisters would talk about sex all the time. They were young and they were curious about all the new and bewildering yearnings their bodies could feel. They had one girlfriend who'd gotten pregnant and had to leave school. And another who had tested positive for HIV.

Sex was so tempting. And yet they understood it could also be dangerous, that it had consequences, serious ones. They had formed a pact, the three of them. They called themselves the NATWC—the Never All the Way Club. Whenever one of them would go off to be alone with a boy, a sister was always somewhere nearby to raise a fist in the air and announce with pride, "NATWC!"

It had worked. They all three remained full-fledged members of the NATWC—at least until college and then...

Well, even triplets, at some point, have to make their own decisions about love and sex and how far to go.

Elli made a turn, toward the river. She parked beneath a cottonwood and she got out and climbed the levee. Hauk, of course, got out, too. He followed in her wake, a shadow—always with her, never speaking.

The mosquitoes were still out. As usual, they found her delicious. She slapped at them now and then. Sometimes she got them—and sometimes not. The ground beneath her sandals was soft. The wild grasses, still moist and green in early May, brushed at her ankles as she climbed.

She reached the crest of the levee. It stretched out, a wide path, in either direction. Below, by the light of the fading last-quarter moon, the river looked dark and oily, flowing easily along. There were dangers, beneath the surface. Swirling currents. Undertows.

But from here, it looked so serene and slow. Hauk stood beside her. As usual, he made no sound. She couldn't even hear him breathing.

She turned in the opposite direction and started walking. He came along behind her, but several yards back, as if he wanted to give her as much space, as much leeway, as he could and still follow the orders he'd been given by his king.

She stopped. Looked at her watch. Ten o'clock.

Hauk came up beside her. She sent him a sad smile. "I know. It's not your fault. None of this. You can't be who you are and behave any differently."

He said nothing. He stared out over the smooth-moving water.

"Come on," she said. "We'll go back now."

When they got to her apartment, the princess wanted a bath. She asked nicely for an hour to herself in the bathroom.

Hauk wanted to shout *No*. He wanted to order her to come with him. Now. Out of here, to the airport, to the jet that awaited her.

But he'd demanded that they leave so many times already. She always refused. And then there was nothing more he could do. He had no rights here. He was to wait and to watch. And then tomorrow, if she continued to balk, he was to use force to see that she went where she'd agreed to go.

In answer to her request for time alone in the bath, he gave her a grunt and a shrug. He wasn't talking to her, hadn't for hours now. Talking to her only led to trouble.

She was too good with that mouth of hers. Whenever he let himself engage in discourse with her, she always got him thinking things he knew he shouldn't let himself think. She would lure him close to doubting the wisdom of his own king, to questioning the way things were and had always been.

And beyond the dangerous questions she had him asking himself, there was that other problem, the one that kept getting worse: the way she roused him, as a man. Whenever she spoke, he would watch her full lips moving and wonder what else she could do with that soft mouth and that clever tongue.

She went into her bathroom and he turned for the guest bath. He emptied his bladder, washed his hands and cleaned his teeth. He returned to her bedroom and rolled out his bedding. And then he stood, waiting, all too aware of the scented moistness of the air, constantly turning his mind from the light beneath the bathroom door, from images of her, naked. Wet. That wheat-colored hair curling and damp from the steam that rose upward off the warm water...

By Odin's one eye, he was doing it again.

He ordered his mind off the thought of her, naked.

He pondered the morning, when her time for stalling, for lingering here, would run out. Would she force him to bind her and gag her again, to toss her over his shoulder and carry her out of here as he'd started to do two days and a lifetime ago?

And the larger question: Would he do it if she did?

That he even asked himself that question spoke volumes about what was happening to him. Something had shifted—inside him. Something had changed. Something in his very self, in who he was.

He'd earned, over time, an inner contentment. Born from high stock, but a bastard, he'd been cast down. Both his mother and his father had past kings in their lineage. Had his mother agreed to marry his father, as a child of two old and powerful families, he would have been high jarl. Had his parents been married, he could now look at Princess Elli eye-to-eye. Even should her father have plans to marry her to another, Hauk would still be her equal, he could still court her. He would have a chance at her hand.

But though his mother succumbed to her passion

for his father, she would not marry. She was kvina soldar: a woman warrior. If she married, she would have been forced to give up her warrior status. For a wife to be a warrior was not done. And, as a result, she condemned her son to start from less than nothing.

A warrior's training was brutal. But Hauk had been born with his father's size and his mother's natural physical skill. He'd fought his way forward to the front of the pack. In recent years, he'd thought that he could see his future and that it was good. He'd believed he brought honor to his bastard name.

He had eight more years in the king's service, and then, when his commission was up, there would be money enough. He'd ask a good woman, one only slightly above him—legitimate and jarl, but low jarl, from an unimportant family, a family only a generation or two up from freeman—to marry him.

And his sons and daughters would have a better start, a better chance than he'd had. Thus, the error of one generation found correction in the next. It had all seemed fitting. Right. Good.

Until now.

Until he'd been sent to kidnap the king's daughter.

And ended up trailing after her wherever she went, looking into those deep-blue eyes, listening to that warm, musical voice. Sitting beside her in a darkened theater, across from her at her own table—and in that restaurant tonight…

There had been a candle on the table tonight. In the warm light, her skin had glowed, soft as the petal of some rare pink rose. He had sat and stared and admired up close what such as he should never see except from a careful, formal distance.

It was all a mistake. A huge one, an error in judgment on the part of his king. His king had trusted him.

And no matter that Hauk had yet to touch the woman intimately—would *never* touch the woman intimately—he had betrayed that trust in his heart and his mind.

Betrayed his king. And thus, betrayed the man he had always believed himself to be.

The door to the bathroom opened. The princess emerged wearing the big pink shirt she liked to sleep in. A cloud of sweet steam came out with her. Her face had a clean, scrubbed shine to it. Her hair was slightly damp at the temples, little tendrils of it curling along her soft, moist cheeks.

Desire was a lance, turning in his flesh, twisting ever deeper.

If only she had never dared to speak of it—to talk of it so calmly, in her easy American way. Her words had seared themselves into his brain.

It's an…attraction, that's all. It happens between men and women. It's natural. We don't have to act on it. And if we did—which we won't—*it would be nobody's business but yours and mine….*

She had him thinking, oh yes, she did. Thinking that to have her would be worth everything—his commission, his pride. Possibly even his freedom and his life. Just one night, to touch her everywhere, to put his mouth on all her most secret places, to hear her call out his name.

What was his life, anyway? Who was he? Less than nothing. Fitz. Bastard. With his small hopes of an insignificant future.

The wife he hadn't found yet was ruined for him now. In the distant, empty time to come, he would look down into her face when they mated and think of the woman standing in the doorway now.

Her Highness said, "You can get comfortable. I'm going to bed."

Hauk pulled off his boots and his stockings and went down to his blankets to wait out the endless night.

Chapter Nine

Somehow, though she never expected she would, Elli did go to sleep. If she dreamed, she didn't recall those dreams when she woke. Her eyes popped open at a few minutes after seven on Thursday morning and her first thought, as she stared at her silent bedside clock, was that she'd forgotten to turn on her alarm.

Her second thought was of Hauk.

Hauk. A warmth spread through her. A longing.

She ordered that longing to get lost. Today, they were leaving. By tonight, she'd be in Gullandria. He'd made it clear that once he delivered her to her father, they might never see each other again. And if they did, it would only be in passing. A quick glimpse, from a distance, in some echoing palace room. That, at most. Nothing more.

She sat up. And found him sitting in the straight chair opposite the end of her bed. He had his boots on and his face was just-shaved smooth.

Elli raked her tangled hair back off her forehead. "Imagine running into you here."

"It is Thursday morning."

Irritation sizzled through her at his preemptive tone. "No kidding."

"Rise. Dress and gather your things. The time to go has come."

She folded her hands on top of the blankets and looked down at them. She was thinking that she ought to just do as he said.

Too bad when she raised her head what came out was, "Think again."

As usual, he sat absolutely still. "Why do you insist on playing these endless mind games?" His eyes were like a pair of lasers, slicing through her, cutting deep.

"This is no game. It's only seven. It will be Thursday morning for five more hours."

His expression showed very little. Yet somehow he seemed to seethe where he sat. There was a long, heated moment during which they glared at each other.

Then he stood. "Five hours then. At noon, you will be ready. At 12:00 p.m., exactly, we will walk out your door."

She yanked her shoulders back and shot him her most defiant scowl. "And if I'm *not* ready?"

"Then I'll bind you hand and foot, stuff a kerchief

in your mouth to still your cries and carry you out.''
He turned on his heel and left.

Elli gripped the blankets and told herself she would
not, under any circumstances, jump from the bed and
chase him down the hall screaming obscenities at the
top of her lungs.

Hauk stood in the hall, composing himself. He
wanted to march back in there, wrap his fingers
around her smooth neck and squeeze the defiance
right out of her. But if he touched her, he knew it
wouldn't be strangling she'd get at his hands.

The most important thing, the goal above all, was
to last until noon without laying a finger on her. Then,
one way or another, he'd take her to the airport. The
Gulfstream could make it nonstop to Gullandria.
Within hours, he'd be turning her over to her father,
the king. Once he got free of her—once she wasn't
there every moment, her very presence like a taunt, a
constant reminder of what he'd never have—he could
begin to purge himself of this impossible hunger for
her.

Through the most recent long and sleepless night,
he'd pondered deeply. And by dawn he'd almost convinced himself that, over time, he would again find
the man he had been before Monday—before two
brief days and three cruel nights of following his
king's beautiful daughter everywhere she went. He'd
almost made himself believe that the day would come
when the prospect of the life that lay before him
would be enough to satisfy him again.

Already there was a bright spot to focus on. Never

again would he be forced to spend a night lying so near to her, forbidden to touch.

Elli got dressed, washed her face, combed her hair and brushed on a little blusher and mascara. Hauk was waiting for her in the hallway when she emerged from the bedroom.

She couldn't seem to stop herself from sneering at him. "There you are again. How can I miss you if you won't go away?"

He fell in step behind her. "You will soon have your wish."

She stopped, turned. And all her anger just melted away. There was nothing left but longing.

"Oh, Hauk. I didn't say it was my wish."

They stared at each other. Always a mistake, for them to stare at each other...

Elli sucked in a trembling breath. "Breakfast," she said. "We need breakfast."

"Yes," he said. "Breakfast."

Neither of them moved.

"Go on," he said.

Somehow, she did it. She turned from those eyes of his and went on down the hall.

The dishwasher was full of clean dishes. Hauk emptied it and set the table. Elli made the coffee, fried the last of the bacon and whipped up some batter for pancakes.

They ate in silence.

And not an angry silence, either. Just a cautious one—cautious and a little bit sad. Elli let her gaze stray out the window to the patch of blue sky between the buildings.

She looked back at Hauk, who was so carefully not looking at her.

Oh, really, he was very dear. He was true and good and…straight-ahead. Not to mention absolutely thrilling to look at. She remembered the little redhead in the restaurant last night. *Is that* yours? *Oh, my, my…*

Elli agreed with the redhead. What woman wouldn't want to make love with Hauk? All that beautiful bronze skin and those big, hard muscles. And those eyes…

Once she'd thought his eyes cold and hard. But she'd learned better in the last two days. His eyes were clear. Unflinching. They spoke of the honesty and strength within.

And it wasn't only that just looking at him made her want to throw herself into those huge arms of his. There was also an odd and lovely… comfortableness, between them. Or at least, there was whenever she let down her guard and stopped manufacturing anger to keep her feelings for him at bay.

Really, other than held tight in his arms, there was no place she'd rather be than right here, at the breakfast table, with Hauk sitting across from her.

How could that have happened, in little more than two days? How had he gone from a terrifying stranger, her kidnapper—to this? The man most likely to turn her knees to jelly, the man she wanted so much to kiss. The man who could clear her table and empty her dishwasher any time, no questions asked.

She set down her fork. "Hauk?"

He allowed himself to look at her.

"Why are we doing this?"

"Because you refuse to give up your stalling and pack your—"

"No."

He looked at her sideways, suspicious.

"Hauk, I don't mean that. I don't mean my going or not going. I mean…you and me. I mean, well, that I *care* for you. A lot." He stared—and he blinked. She waved a hand. "Oh, I know. It sounds crazy, to say that, considering why you came here in the first place, considering that it's only been a couple of days since we met. But so what if it's crazy? It's also true. I do care for you. And I think you care for me." He was gaping at her. He looked utterly stunned. She continued. "I don't see why we can't just—"

"Enough." Hauk dropped his own fork. It clattered to his plate.

"But I want you to—"

His chair screeched across the floor tiles as he surged to his feet. "I have told you. I know you have heard. There can be nothing between us. Ever."

She looked up at him unblinking. "That is so ridiculous."

"To you, perhaps."

"No. Not only to me. To any…thinking individual."

"Now you insult my intelligence."

"No, I'm not. You know I'm not. And we both know what *you're* doing now. You're trying to drum up some fake reason to be angry with me—and I don't blame you for doing that. I mean, it's not as if

I haven't been doing it, too. But we both know it's all just an act, just a hopeless attempt on both our parts to keep from admitting how we really feel about each other.''

He fell back a step—as if he needed all the distance from her he could get, as if he feared she might actually reach out and touch him.

She did no such thing—she didn't even move. ''You think of me as a princess, as someone far above you, someone out of your reach. But that's...all in your mind. I'm no princess. Not really. You're always telling me that I think like an American. Well, that's because, as *I* keep telling you, I *am* an American. I might have been born in Gullandria, but I've lived all but the first ten months of my life right here, in Sacramento. The laws and customs of Gullandria don't apply to me. At heart, where it matters, I'm just Elli Thorson. And I think, honestly, that we might have something here, you and me. Something really powerful. Something so good...''

Apparently, he didn't agree with her. He stood to attention now. He was just waiting for her to be done with him. Waiting so that he could go.

''Oh, Hauk,'' she said in a low voice.

''Are you finished?''

She bit her lip, gave a small, hopeless shrug.

To get away from her, out of the kitchen, he had to go past her. It was his undoing.

She caught his wrist as he tried to get by. ''Oh, Hauk. Please...''

He froze. The air seemed to shimmer around them. Heat radiated from the point where her flesh touched his. That heat was spreading out, all through her body. Arrows of longing zinged straight through her heart.

She had a split second—even less than that—and he would shake her off. She didn't give him time to do it. She swept upward, out of her chair, throwing her arms around his neck, pressing her body against his big, hard chest.

It was too much for him. His resistance broke. With a low moan he gathered her close.

Stunned that she'd gotten exactly what she'd yearned for, Elli stared upward, into his wonderful, square-jawed, determined face.

Oh, my. This was a lovely, lovely place to be, held so close against his heart, those huge, strong arms wrapped around her.

He whispered, "You should not have touched me."

"Oh, right. Ask me not to breathe, while you're at it."

"You should not—"

"Shh." She slid one hand up between their bodies, put two fingers against his mouth. "Stop that," she chided, oh so tenderly.

His mouth moved. She felt his breath flow down her hand. His lips parted slightly and his lower teeth scraped her finger pads.

Elli shivered—with delight, with excitement. "Oh, see? See, this is how it *ought* to be...."

His big hand was in her hair. He cupped the back of her head. "A mistake. This is all a dangerous mistake."

"Stop that. You stop that right now. This is no

mistake. I just told you what this is. This is how it ought to be.'' She was pressed very close to him, close enough to feel his arousal—and to revel in it. In her own most intimate place, she felt…hollowed out, moist and needful and longing to be filled with him. She gasped. ''Oh, Hauk. Kiss me. Kiss me, please.''

Her eyes drifted closed.

Hauk looked down at that beautiful mouth, the mouth she offered, the mouth she wanted him to have.

Damned, he thought. *I am damned to the bitter cold and unending night of Hel, to do this.*

But right at that moment, he didn't care. He thought, *Just the taste of her. Why shouldn't I have that? She wants me to have that. Only a taste….*

Her head tipped back, her mouth tipped up. She loosed the sweetest, tiniest sigh.

He thought, *Only that. One kiss. And that sigh, inside me, all the rest of my days.*

He brought his mouth down over hers.

Her lips parted. The sweetness within nearly finished him—right there, in her kitchen, in the bright light of morning. He tasted the slick inner surface beyond her soft lips and he thought he was dying.

An acceptable sacrifice, the loss of his life. He was glad to go, though Valhalla would be lost to him— ah, the shame of it.

The king's warrior, dead in a kitchen of a woman's kiss…

He held her more tightly, his hands roaming her slim back, pressing that softness, that female warmth all the closer. Those full breasts of hers pushed against his chest. She moaned and her breath, sweet and hot and scented of coffee, flowed into his mouth. He sucked it in all the deeper, down into his soul. He would keep it forever, along with her sigh.

Her soft fingers danced at the nape of his neck, threading into his hair, caressing outward, across his shoulders, then sliding back to clasp around his neck again. Her tongue, shy at first, grew bolder, darting into his mouth, flicking along the top of his own tongue, pausing there, darting back.

She made a small, hungry sound, like a kitten seeking strokes. He groaned in response. And he swept his hands downward, over the incredible twin swells of her bottom, tucking her into him, his manhood pressing her most secret place.

He was so hard. His body commanded him. To lay her down, to make her his...

He curved the slim length of her backward over his arm, and he lost her mouth in order to gain the petal-soft flesh of her sweet chin, to run his tongue down the glorious stretch of her long, satiny throat.

"Oh, Hauk. Oh, yes, yes..." She pressed her hips up against him, in invitation, in a promise of something he knew he couldn't take.

Yet still, she promised. She promised him everything. She murmured sweet encouragements, she drove him on with sighs.

He kissed the twin points of her collarbone, pausing there, where her pulse beat in the hollow of her throat, to breathe deep, to suck in the womanly, flower-sweet scent of her, adding it to the treasures he'd already claimed—that sigh before he kissed her, that later breath. Breath upon breath, he would have them all.

Those soft hands of hers were at his waist, fumbling with the shirt he wore, gathering it, sliding it upward. She caressed the bare skin over his ribs, scratching him lightly, tauntingly, with her fingernails.

He nuzzled the fabric of her light cotton blouse, burying his face in the soft swell of a breast, finding her nipple beneath the layers of clothing.

He teased that nipple, drawing it up to a point, then closing his mouth over it, sending out a focused breath of air across it, biting at it, lightly, feeling it pebble up more firmly, as if it begged for more.

She'd forgotten her task of removing his shirt. Her hand splayed in his hair now, pressing him closer, against her offered breast. He latched on, sucking, soaking the fabric over her nipple as he toyed with it.

"Oh, yes," she moaned, pulling him ever closer. "Oh, yes, yes, yes, yes…"

He brought one hand between them, laid it in the center of her chest, against the glorious fullness of those proud breasts.

"Yes…" She urged him on, soft lips against his ear, warm breath against his skin. She captured his earlobe, teased it between her teeth. "Yes, Hauk. Oh, yes…" Her hips moved against his, promising untold delights.

Offering everything.

All of her. All she was, all she had. So much. More than he had ever dared to dream of in his bastard soul.

A prize beyond measure. Worth any price. He found the first button on her blouse, captured it between his thumb and his forefinger.

"Yes," she whispered, one more time.

And then the phone rang.

Chapter Ten

The jarring bleat of the phone ruined everything.

Hauk went still as a statue in Elli's arms.

She gripped his big shoulders and begged him, "Oh, please, just let it ring."

But he was already taking her hands, gently peeling them away, his face flushed and regretful, shaking his head. "We must stop. You know that."

"No, I don't know that. I don't know that at all."

He stepped back from her. She had that feeling of something tearing again, as in the movie theater the day before. Only worse. A thousand times worse.

He said softly, "Answer the phone."

She wanted to scream, to throw something. "No."

"Don't behave like a spoiled child."

He was right and she knew it.

Not about having to stop—never, ever about that.

She had given up fighting this lovely, impossible magic between them. And she was furious with him all over again, to look in his face and see his jaw was set—like his mind—against her, against what might be between them, against all they might share.

But acting out wouldn't solve anything. She went to the counter and punched the button that answered the call on speakerphone. "Hello?"

"Elli. Oh, sweetheart…"

"Aunt Nanna." Like her daughters, Elli's mother had been one of fraternal triplets. Elli's Aunt Kirsten lived in San Francisco. Aunt Nanna lived in Napa. There had been a brother, too, but he had died when Elli and her sisters were babies.

Nanna made a worried noise, low in her throat. "I was afraid…"

"Afraid of what?"

"That you'd already have gone."

Elli shut her eyes and tried to collect her scattered wits, to concentrate on what her aunt was saying instead of thinking of what hadn't quite had a chance to happen between her and Hauk. "I, uh, take it you've been talking to Mom?"

"Oh, Elli. I just got off the phone with her."

Elli opened her eyes and there he was, watching. She turned away, toward the window, so she wouldn't have to look at him. "I'll be leaving in a few hours."

"Oh, honey, are you absolutely sure about this?"

"Yes. I'm positive." And she was. Positive about a lot more than just the trip to meet her father.

"Ingrid's so worried for you. I am, too. You don't really understand the way things work in that place.

I'm sorry to say it, but your father is not a man anyone should trust. He broke your mother's heart, you know, he broke—''

Elli had heard it all before. ''Nanna, what, exactly, did he *do* that's made you all hate him so?''

Nanna took a moment to answer. Elli could just see her, pursing up her mouth. Finally she said, ''You'll have to speak with your mother about that.''

''That's what you always say. And when I ask Mom, I get nothing. So let's just leave it, okay? Accept the fact that I have to meet him, to decide how I feel about him for myself.''

Nanna made a small, frustrated sound.

Elli said firmly, ''I want to do this, I sincerely do.''

Nanna sighed. ''Your mother warned me that there'd be no way to change your mind.''

''And she was right—how's Uncle Cam?'' Her uncle was a total type A. He'd had a quadruple bypass a couple of months ago.

''Elli—''

''Come on, Aunt Nanna. I'm going and that's all there is to it. So how's Uncle Cam?''

The silence that followed told Elli her aunt was debating with herself—to let it be as Elli asked. Or to press on with her warnings and her worries.

Nanna let it be. ''Your Uncle Cam is doing well. We've got him eating low-salt and low-fat. He's taking his medication....''

They talked for a few more minutes, about her cousins, Nanna's son and daughter, who were both in high school, about Elli's two classes of bright-eyed kindergartners. Elli promised she'd make it over to Napa at least once during her summer break.

"Take care," Nanna said at last. "Be safe."

"I love you. I will."

The line went dead and after a second or two, the dial tone buzzed. Hauk was the one who reached out and pressed the button to cut off the sound. Elli turned from the window and met his eyes. Distant eyes now. Once again, he had barricaded his heart behind a shield of watchfulness. Looking at his stern, unforgiving face, she wanted to throw herself against him, to beat on his broad chest, to demand that he show her his real, tender self again.

Her shirt was wet, where he'd put his mouth to her breast. She looked down at it, at the moist circle over her right nipple. Then, proudly, she lifted her head.

"Guess I'd better change my shirt."

"Pack," he said. The single word echoed harshly, like a door slamming shut.

What more could she say, except, "Yes. I guess I'd better do that."

For once, he didn't fall in behind her as she turned for the hall. Great, she thought. She could use a break. A few precious minutes to herself, to get past her shameless disappointment at losing her chance to get lost in his arms.

Elli paused in the doorway to her bedroom. She leaned her forehead against the doorframe and shut her eyes and wished it didn't have to be like this.

Maybe she should just look on the bright side. At least for a few unforgettable minutes there, she'd had a taste of what it might be like to be Hauk Fitz-Wyborn's love....

Elli drew herself up. Really, looking on the bright side just wasn't going to cut it. She unbuttoned the shirt that was still wet from his kiss and went to the bathroom to toss it in the hamper.

Okay, so he'd been saved by the bell. This time.

In her bedroom, she pushed open her closet door.

He still had a commitment to escort her to Gullandria. And after they got there, she might find ways to see him, to be near him.

She took a jewel-blue silk shirt from a hanger, put her arms in the sleeves and buttoned it up.

Why not think positively? She wanted him, she *cared* for him. And as hard as he kept fighting it, she believed in her heart that he wanted and cared for her, too.

He'd let down his guard once. It could happen again. Maybe she'd get another chance to show him just how strongly she felt for him. And maybe next time, he wouldn't push her away.

She got her big suitcase and hoisted it to the bed, laying it open. Standing very still, she listened. She heard nothing. Hauk could move so quietly. He might be standing in the doorway right now.

She shot a glance over her shoulder.

Empty.

Good. She listened some more and ended up deciding she felt reasonably certain he'd yet to leave the kitchen. He didn't want to be near her right now. He needed a little time to marshal his defenses against her.

Suited her just fine.

She went to the tall dresser by the inner wall and pulled open the top drawer—all the way open, so she could get to the very back of it.

Her hand closed on the box that she'd pushed in there a few months ago. She'd been dating someone then, on a regular basis. She'd thought that maybe it might become more than it was.

But the relationship had cooled before it ever really heated up. In the meantime, though, she'd bought the box of condoms, just in case.

Right now, with Hauk, it was much more than a *just in case* situation. If a miracle happened and he held out his arms to her, she would run to him, eagerly. Better safe than sorry, if her dreams did come true.

At ten-thirty, she was ready to go. She got her passport from the desk in the spare room. She was slipping it into her purse when Hauk appeared in the doorway.

"Are you ready?"

She thought of the box of condoms and she almost let out a wild little laugh. "Um-hm."

"Your suitcase?"

"In my bedroom."

He turned toward the door to her room.

She followed behind him. "I packed my overnighter, too. And I can carry both bags myself, honestly. The big one has those rollers and…" She let her voice trail off. There was no point in saying more.

He slung the strap of the smaller bag over his

shoulder and he grabbed the handle of the big suitcase and headed for the front door.

Fine. Let him haul it all down the stairs by himself if he wanted to. She checked the lock on the patio door and made sure all the lights were out. He waited for her by the front door, laden with her bags and that big black duffel of his, too.

She opened the door and gestured him out ahead of her. At the base of the stairs, she turned for the carports.

"No," he said. "Follow me." He led her out another way, to a side street and a black van.

"Tinted windows," she remarked. "An absolute necessity when it comes to kidnapping unwilling princesses."

It was a bad joke and it fell flat. He didn't bother to respond.

She just couldn't leave it at that. "I suppose you'll want me to drive. You'll need your hands free to keep me under control. Then again, who knows? If I'm behind the wheel, I could go wild, decide to make a break for Bakersfield."

He was already turning for the driver's door himself. "Just get in."

Her father's Gulfstream jet had a roomy pressurized cabin furnished with six high-backed leather seats, teak tables beside them. There were also a collapsible dividing wall and a full-size bed that could be pulled down to make the divided-off space into a flying bedroom.

"Does Your Highness wish a nap?" the attendant

inquired. She was a tall blonde in a slim black skirt and a crisp white shirt. She had a blue-and-gold lightning bolt embroidered on her pocket as well as on the crest of her jaunty-looking red garrison cap.

"No, thanks." Elli took one of the high-backed leather chairs as Hauk, shoulders hunched, golden head grazing the ceiling, moved farther down the cabin.

"Refreshment?"

"Not right now." Elli's mind wasn't on food. She resisted the urge to lean out of her seat and look back at Hauk. He'd been depressingly silent on the drive to the airport—not that his silence was anything all that new or different. It only seemed that way, after those beautiful, too-brief moments in his arms.

"Fasten your seatbelt," said the flight attendant. "We'll be cleared for takeoff soon."

Elli nodded and smiled and the attendant left her alone. She looked out the window as they taxied along the runway. It all seemed so…civilized, the attractive attendant, the beautifully appointed jet. She couldn't help wondering what the attendant might have said to her had Hauk brought her on board all tied up with a gag in her mouth.

Probably nothing. The woman would have pulled the collapsible divider across the cabin and brought down the bed and Hauk would have dropped Elli on it without anyone asking if she'd care for a nap.

It would be a long flight, but it would be nonstop. Hauk sat in his seat and tried not to stare at her seat in front of him. The sky out the window was clear. Fat white clouds drifted below the wing.

It was over—their time together. In the end, his sense of duty and his understanding of his place in the world had triumphed. He hadn't succumbed to the desperate hunger that would have caused her nothing but shame and heartache and cost him more than he cared to contemplate. He told himself he was glad it had gone no further between them.

An indiscreet embrace and a few passionate kisses—more than he should have allowed to happen. But not total disaster. Thanks to a ringing phone, he'd stopped it in time.

He was weary. Of everything. Hauk shut his eyes and allowed himself to disappear into the first deep sleep he'd known in days.

He woke, startled, when the plane dropped several hundred feet and then slammed against an air current below.

The attendant, in a chair down near the cockpit door, wore a bright, professional smile. "A little turbulence. Nothing to worry about."

He took her at her word, at first. But the going got rougher, the plane rising and dropping like a toy in the hands of a brutal child. Rain drove against the windows. The sky beyond the insulated panes was black a few feet from the glass—except when Thor threw his hammer and lightning in ragged fingers lit the blackness with a golden-green light, followed not long after by the deafening crack and roll of thunder.

Hauk got up and worked his way forward. He

paused by the seat of the princess—after all, it was his duty to check on her. To keep her safe.

She looked up at him. "Kind of rough, huh?"

"You're all right?"

She gave him a nod. "I'm good." It was another reason among the thousand reasons that she was a woman any man would covet—she didn't frighten easily.

Lightning speared through the blackness outside again, its eerie glow suffusing the cabin. Thunder boomed. The plane dropped sharply, then bottomed out hard against the fist of a rising air current.

And through it all, he stared at her and she looked up at him, her face pale and calm and so beautiful it felled him like a deathblow from an enemy's ax. "I'll check our status with the pilot."

She nodded, shifted that haunting gaze away. He staggered on toward the cockpit.

The pilot told him what he'd already deduced. There was no fighting through this mess. They no longer had the fuel to make it all the way to Gullandria. They would have to land, refuel and then wait for the storm to blow itself out.

It was, to say the least, a rocky next few hours. Elli was never so grateful as when Hauk told her they'd gotten the go-ahead to land at a private airstrip just outside of Boston.

The landing was one of those lurching, scary, hope-I-never-do-this-again kind of experiences. But they made it and they made it safely. As soon as the plane taxied to a stop, Hauk went forward a second time to speak with the pilot.

He came out looking bleak. "The storm shows no signs of abating. This will be an overnight stop."

"Will we just stay here, on the plane?"

He shook his head. "I'll arrange for suitable lodging."

Lodging. A triumphant little thrill shot through her. Hauk wouldn't be rid of her quite as soon as he'd hoped.

And so very much might happen, in one more night alone together....

Half an hour later, Elli looked out the window and saw a long, black limousine rolling across the tarmac toward the jet.

"Will you have need of both your suitcases?" Hauk asked, his tone carefully formal.

Elli had flown enough to be prepared for situations like this. "Just the smaller one."

"Your Highness." The flight attendant presented her with a big black umbrella at the cabin door.

"Thanks." The rain was coming down in sheets, the wind gusting hard.

Halfway down the steps, the umbrella turned inside out. Hauk, right behind her, took it from her hand. He shouted against the gale, his voice hearty with sudden good humor, "Speed will serve you better than this." He held the ruined umbrella high. Already, that golden hair was plastered to his head. Water ran off his bladelike nose. His eyes gleamed. Apparently, he liked wild weather—enough that he'd even forgotten for a moment to treat her like the princess he didn't dare to touch. ''Run!''

She took off down the final steps and sprinted across the streaming pavement to the open door of the limousine. Hauk ducked in right after her, pulling the door shut, tossing the useless umbrella to the floor. They waited a moment or two, while the necessary bags were stowed in the trunk. And then they were off.

Their hotel suite was on the thirty-fifth floor, with a view of the harbor where the storm was tossing all the boats around. There were two big bedrooms, each with its own bath, a living and dining area between. Elli suppressed a knowing smile when she saw there was a second bedroom. Wishful thinking on Hauk's part. The poor man. Duty bound to sleep wherever she did.

Oh, yes. It could turn out to be a very interesting night.

They ate dinner in the room. Elli hadn't realized how hungry she was until the bellhop wheeled it in. She'd ordered the pheasant. It was absolutely wonderful.

For dessert, she had amaretto crème brûlée. It was practically sexual, how delicious it tasted. She ate every last creamy bit.

Hauk, on the other hand, seemed to have little appetite. He mostly sat and watched her. He was looking broody again.

She could almost feel sorry for him.

A whole night of temptation ahead. How *would* he get through it?

Ah, well. She'd do her very best to help him with that.

She sent him a bright smile. "Does my father know we're going to be a day late?"

He nodded. "The message has been sent."

Via the mysterious black beeper thingy, no doubt. "Well, good. I wouldn't want him to worry."

Hauk narrowed his eyes at her. "You are much too cheerful."

She toasted him with the last of her wine—he, of course, wasn't having any. "You'd rather I scowled and brooded like you?"

"You have some scheme you're hatching."

"You are just so suspicious."

"Not without good cause."

"What can I tell you? I was born in Gullandria and Osrik Thorson is my father. Scheming comes as naturally to me as...tying people up does to you." She drank and set the empty glass down.

He said, thoughtfully, "It takes study and practice to master the secrets in a strong length of rope."

She looked at him sideways. "Now, why did that sound like some kind of veiled threat?"

He drank from his water glass. "I am your servant. Never would I threaten you." He set the glass down and pushed back his chair. "I bid you good night."

It took her a moment to absorb what he'd just told her. He'd already grabbed that black duffel of his from where he'd left it in the corner and strode to the door of one of the bedrooms before she stopped him.

"Hauk."

He turned, put his fist to his chest and dipped his head. "At your service."

"What are you doing?"

"Going to bed."

"But I'm...not ready for bed yet. I want a long bath first."

"By all means, have your bath. Watch the television from your bed as you enjoy doing. This is America. There's a television in every room."

She didn't like what she thought might be happening here. "Then we are, uh, sleeping in separate rooms tonight?"

"Yes."

She had an awful, sinking feeling. All her glorious and naughty plans to seduce him were destined to come to nothing, after all. Disappointment had her dishing out a mean-spirited taunt. "You do serve me. I could command you to sleep at the foot of my bed."

"Yes. But that would be needlessly cruel and you are not that kind of woman."

Her throat felt tight. She swallowed. "Hauk?"

"Yes?"

"You would rather take a chance that I might run away than sleep in the same room with me tonight?"

He didn't answer. He didn't have to.

She felt ashamed. "I won't run away—wherever you sleep."

There was a long moment where neither of them spoke. Rain beat against the wide window that looked out on the lights of Boston and the harbor beyond. Lightning jumped and flashed across the black sky.

Elli felt that something very precious, a onetime chance that would never come again, was slipping away.

"All right," she said at last. "Good night, then."

He turned and went through the door to the bedroom, closing it quietly behind him.

Hauk tossed his duffel on the bed and strode to the bathroom, pulling off his clothes as he went. He turned on the shower and stepped into the stall with the water running cold.

It wasn't cold enough. It could never be cold enough. The ice-crusted Sherynborn—the river that ran through the Vildelund at home—in dead of winter wouldn't be cold enough.

He stayed in there for a long time. It didn't help, not in any measurable way. It didn't cure him of the yearning that was eating him alive. But the beating of the cool water on his skin provided something of a distraction, at least.

When he got out, he toweled dry and then he spent an hour on the dragon dials, a series of strenuous exercises consisting of slow, controlled movements combined with precise use of the breath. He'd learned the dials at his mother's knee. There were, after all, *some* benefits to being born the bastard of a well-trained and highly skilled woman warrior. Fighting women took great pains to develop control and flexibility in order to make up for their lesser physical strength. A woman warrior sometime in the 17th century had created the discipline of the dials.

All his life, the dials had served him well. They

brought him physical exhaustion and mental clarity, always.

But not tonight. Nothing seemed to help him tonight.

He showered again—quickly this time—to wash off the sweat. Then he stood in the middle of the bedroom and stared at the shut door to the central living area and tried not to think how easy it would be to pull it open, to stride across the space between his room and hers.

A knock and she would answer. She would open her arms to him. She had made that so very, very clear.

Somehow, he kept his hand from reaching for the door. He climbed naked into the bed with thoughts that were scattered. Wild.

He stared toward the window opposite the foot of the bed. He'd left the blinds open. The rain beat against the single wide pane, streaming down in glittering trails, like veils of liquid jewels. When the lightning speared through the sky, the room would flash as bright as day. He tried to concentrate on that, on the beauty of the storm.

But he was not successful. Images of the woman kept haunting him. He arrived, constantly, at the point of thinking her name.

He'd already deliberately disobeyed his king, left her to her own devices for this entire night. She might turn and run. He'd have to track her down, or it would not go well for him.

But she'd said she wouldn't run. And in his heart, he believed her.

The chance she might flee was not the true problem here. His climbing from this bed and going to her—that was the problem.

His own mind, usually a model of order and discipline, betrayed him now. It mattered not what orders he gave it, it *would* continue straying to forbidden thoughts of what it might be like, for just one night, to call her his love.

He lay there and he stared into the darkness. He listened to the storm raging outside and he tried not to see her face, not to think her forbidden name.

And in the end, it was as if all his efforts to deny her had only conjured her to come to him.

There was a soft knock at the door.

It fell to him to call out, *Go away.*

But he said nothing. He lay there. Waiting.

Slowly, the door opened and there she was in her big pink shirt.

He sat up. And he said the word he'd vowed to himself that he would never say—her name, unadorned.

"Elli."

Chapter Eleven

Elli.

It was the first time, ever, that he'd called her by her given name alone. Her chest felt too small, suddenly, to hold her hungry heart.

The light from the room behind her spilled in across the bed. The blankets covered him to the waist.

He was…so beautiful and savage to her civilized eyes, with his broad smooth chest and the lightning-bolt tattoo slashing across it through a thicket of vines and dragons and swords. And his eyes… Oh, they were the saddest, loneliest eyes she'd ever seen.

"Hauk, is it all right if I come in?" Even now, after he'd at last dared to call her Elli, she more or less expected him to send her away.

But what she dreaded didn't happen. Instead, he flicked on the lamp beside him and held out his hand.

With a glad cry, she ran for the bed and scrambled up onto it, aiming straight for his arms. He wrapped them around her with an eagerness that warmed her to her soul. He stretched out on his back and she settled against him, cuddling close, with only his blankets and her big shirt between them now. She laid her head against his heart and noted with a surge of slightly silly joy that it seemed to beat right in time with hers.

She felt his lips brush the crown of her head. And she snuggled even closer with a long, happy sigh.

"Maybe I'll never move," she threatened tenderly. "I'll just lie here, forever, holding on to you...."

Hauk made a low sound in his throat and kissed her hair again. Most important, he kept those warm strong arms around her. How absolutely lovely. To rest in his embrace, to feel his kiss in her hair, his heart beating a little fast like her own, but steady and true, too, under her ear.

She spoke dreamily, without lifting her head. "Hauk, you probably won't believe this, but I came in here to *talk* to you."

"Ah," he said. "To talk. Always a danger, when *you* want to talk."

She faked an outraged cry and lightly punched his arm.

He stroked her hair. "Go ahead then. Say what you came to say."

She lifted her head. "I want to suggest something to you. And I want you to really think about it before you tell me it's not possible...." He was looking at her. And she was looking back at him. And suddenly what she'd intended to say was the last thing on her mind. "Oh, Hauk…"

He said her name again, "Elli…" The sound thrilled her.

With a hungry cry, she scooted up the glorious terrain of his big body to claim those beautiful lips.

Lightning flashed and thunder rolled as her mouth touched his. Elli didn't know or care which storm—the one outside or the sweeter, hotter one between them—had caused the bright pulsing behind her eyelids, the lovely, echoing, booming crash that seemed to shake her to the core. She kissed him harder, longer, deeper.

And he didn't hold back. He kissed her tenderly, passionately. He made her stomach hollow out and all her thoughts melt away to nothing but joy and a longing to be his. She rubbed herself against him, shamelessly eager, and she felt his response to her, knew that he was ready, so ready, to be hers.

But then he was capturing her chin, making her look at him. "We are foolish, *worse* than foolish."

She couldn't argue fast enough. "Oh, no. That's not so. Everything will work out. Just you wait and see."

His fine mouth curved upward. "You are, truly, an American."

She was so delighted to see his expression, she forgot to be irked at his superior tone. "Oh, Hauk. Look at that. I swear that's a smile you've got on your mouth."

"What man wouldn't smile after kissing you?"

She touched his lips, so soft when the rest of him

was anything but. So soft and so perfectly designed for kissing…

"Oh, Hauk…" Her eyes drifted closed and she lifted her mouth to him.

But just before her lips touched his and all rational thought could fly away, she remembered that she had something important to tell him. Her eyes popped open. "Wait."

He actually chuckled. "What?"

She kissed the ridge of a crescent-shaped scar on his chin, because she couldn't resist the temptation. But then she did pull back enough to say, "I was lying in that big, lonely bed in the other room, thinking…"

He raised his huge arms, laced his fingers behind his head and lifted one eyebrow. "About?"

She canted up on an elbow and laid a hand on his smooth chest, right in the center, where the lightning bolt zagged and a dragon reared, breathing fire. "My father."

He didn't move. That one eyebrow was still arched, yet it seemed to her that his rare lighthearted mood had vanished as swiftly as the sun sliding behind a dark cloud. Lightning flared again, a blinding glare through the room, and somewhere out in the storm-dark sky, thunder boomed and rolled away.

"Just listen to what I have to say." She touched the hard line of his jaw. "Please."

"I'm listening."

"Everyone—my mother, my sisters, Hildy, Aunt Nanna and you, too—you all seem to think my father has something else planned for me. That there's more going on here than a father's desire to meet a daughter he's never really known.''

''I never said—''

''Bear with me. Please?''

He gave her a curt nod.

She spoke briskly. ''So, then, what could it be, this other reason he's sent for me?''

''We've spoken of this.'' His gaze slid away. ''I've told you I don't know.''

She reached up again, this time to touch his cheek. ''Don't look away....''

He unlaced his fingers and dropped one hand at his side. The other hand he rested in the curve of her back—but very lightly, as if he didn't plan on keeping it there for long. ''All right.'' He was frowning. ''I'll say it once more. I can't tell you what His Majesty has planned for you, if anything, beyond what we already know—a time to speak with you, to see your face, to know the splendid young woman his infant daughter has become.''

''Splendid, huh? I like the sound of that.''

''It's only the truth.''

She trailed her hand down, so tenderly, and rested it once more against the dragon's heart. ''I think you do suspect his plans, Hauk.''

''It is not my place to—''

''Don't say it.'' She put her fingers to his lips. ''I don't need to hear it again. I sincerely do not.''

He moved his head, to free his mouth from her shushing hand. ''What do you wish me to say?''

''Nothing. Just listen.''

He gazed at her coolly now. She wondered if this

conversation would cost her the precious night to come.

No. She wouldn't think that way. Once he heard what she had to tell him, he would cradle her close and kiss her, again and again. They'd hold back the dawn together.

And morning would find them all wrapped up in each other's arms.

"Hauk, I think my father has plans for me—wedding plans. I think you think so, too, and—" She cut herself off with a tiny cry of distress. "Oh, don't do that, don't…get that hard and distant look."

"Why say such a thing?" His voice was ragged. "Why say it now, except to remind me that I betray my king—and that you and I have nothing beyond this moment, this moment that shouldn't even be?"

"No. No, you don't understand. You have to let me finish."

"What do you want from me?" He dragged himself up against the padded headboard, took her by the shoulders and pushed her carefully away from him.

"I said, let me finish." Elli had gathered her legs beneath her. She knelt beside him, her hands folded tightly on her thighs. He didn't want her to touch him right then, that was painfully evident in every line of his face, every tense muscle in his beautiful body. Clasping her hands together was the only way she could make them behave.

"All right, then," he said way too quietly. "Finish."

"Oh, don't you see? Why would he send you here, why would he force us to be together every minute?

Unless he's hoping I'll see just what I see in you,
unless it's *you* he's hoping I'll learn to love and want
to marry?''

When she said that, Hauk's hurt and anger melted
away like the snowfields over Drakveden Fjord in the
spring.

He almost smiled again. No matter that this woman
was his king's daughter, in her heart she was American. American to the core. She saw what she wanted
to see. She made the world over to fit her own idea
of it.

Those deep-blue eyes of hers were shining. By all
the roots of the guardian tree, he hadn't the will or
the heart to remind her of the facts. Somewhere in
that sharp mind of hers, she had to know the truth.
That he'd first been sent to take her quickly and bring
her straight to his king. That it was *she,* with her
insistence on speaking to her father, on striking a bargain, who had made it necessary for Hauk to assume
the role of round-the-clock guard.

Why point out the obvious when she so clearly
didn't want to see it? Why be wise now, when for
once in his life, all he wanted was a chance to play
the fool?

The mighty Thor, her family's namesake, most beloved of all the gods, had given him this night of
driving rain and rolling thunder, had forced her father's ship out of the sky. Sometimes, the whims of
the gods might favor a man.

For an hour. Or a night.

A man might, however briefly, hold in his arms his
greatest desire.

In the morning, there would be time for wisdom, for acceptance.

For regret and for anger.

And for shame, as well.

She whispered, "Are you going to send me away?"

It was the moment to tell her, to make her understand that her wild, bright American dreams would not change what was. If her father did have plans for her to marry a Gullandrian, it wouldn't be his low-jarl bastard warrior he intended for her. It would be the man King Osrik thought most likely to be king himself someday. That way the Thorson bloodline would continue to hold the throne. That way, even if His Majesty had lost his sons, the day might come when his grandson would rule.

"Oh, Hauk…" Those eyes of hers begged him to see what she saw—the two of them, united, His Majesty, her father, blessing the match.

He knew he should make the truth clear, that he should tell her what would really happen if they shared this stormy night and His Majesty found out.

At the very least, Hauk would lose his position, be stripped of all honors. He could be banished or even sent to Tarngalla, the tower prison where murderers and those who committed crimes against the state were kept. It was highly unlikely that what they were doing might cost him his life—not in this modern day and age. But anything could happen when the most trusted of soldiers dared to betray his king.

He knew if he told her all that, she would scoff.

She would call it impossible, barbaric, medieval. She would say it was wrong and unfair and an outrage.

And then she'd return to her own room. Even if she didn't want to believe him, she wouldn't let him take the risk.

Hauk cared nothing for the risk. She was here. She wished to stay. And he was through battling. The war inside him was over—at least for this night. For the brief, lightning-struck hours to come, he would hold this woman in his arms.

She sat there, on her knees, her fine face flushed and hopeful—those slender hands clasped. "Hauk, I…"

"Yes? Tell me."

"If you let me stay…"

"Yes?"

"Well, if you do, then I confess…"

She seemed to need more urging. He gave it. "You confess…"

"Since this morning, when you kissed me and then sent me to my room to pack, I have…thought of this. Hoped for this. Prepared for this."

"Prepared?"

The blush on her cheeks flooded outward, suffusing her entire sweet face with color. "You said you'd never have children until you had a wife."

By the breath of the dragon, he'd said exactly that—and meant it. He'd also taken a blood oath to give undying loyalty to his king. But look at him now.

"I'm a responsible woman." She was earnest now, enchantingly so. "I'd never ask you to go against your beliefs. I have contraception."

Contraception. Of course. American to the core.

She looked so very sincere about this. And so beautiful.

He told her simply, "That's wise." There were other things he might have said. But anything else would have brought questions he saw no need to answer right then.

He wasn't a total thief. He'd only take the taste of her, her deep, warm sighs, the touch of her skin to his. There'd be no risk he'd put a bastard in her belly. She'd understand that, soon enough. They didn't need to talk it over now.

She slid up his chest again and pressed her sweet mouth to his—quickly, this time. And firmly. "I'll go then. I'll…get them." She pretended to glare. "You stay right here."

"Your wish is my command."

She jumped from the bed and hurried to the door, pausing there briefly to send him a tender look. Then she was gone. He lay back, thinking that he loved the lightning. It had always pleased him. And it seemed all the brighter the dimmer the room. He switched off the lamp.

A moment later, she returned, a small box in her hand.

She set the box by the bed.

He whispered, "You don't need that big pink shirt. Not now. Not for the rest of the night."

She hesitated, hovering there beside the bed, the wedge of light from the open door behind her casting her face into shadow, making a halo around her golden hair.

Lightning flared. He saw her face clearly—uncertain and sweetly shy. The light went out. Thunder boomed.

She took the bottom of the shirt, whipped it up and over her head. And tossed it away.

Chapter Twelve

Hauk held back the blanket. Elli slid in beside him. He wrapped the blanket around her and he looked down at her, a look so tender—and yet also somehow infinitely sad.

Apprehension rose within her. "What? What's the matter?" She brushed two fingers along his brow, wishing her touch could soothe away his frown. "Hauk?"

Instead of giving her an answer, he lowered his mouth to hers. His lips touched her lips and her apprehension vanished as if it had never been. And his sadness? Surely, he couldn't be sad now. There was no such thing as sadness—not when he was kissing her, not when they held each other close.

He clasped her waist with his big hand and he kissed his way over her chin and down her throat.

Pushing back the blanket, he raised up over her, resting on an elbow. He looked down at her—at all of her. She gloried in that, in having him look at her. She felt no shyness, no embarrassment. It seemed right that he should see her. She *wanted* him to see her.

It seemed that she could actually feel his gaze, that where he looked, he touched. She shivered in blissful response.

Slowly he lowered his head to her left breast. His hair trailed on her skin. She felt the touch of his tongue—one long, wet swipe, deliciously abrasive, against the yearning flesh of her nipple. And then he blew where he'd licked.

Elli moaned in delight.

He lifted his head again. She looked at him from under lowered lashes and saw his white teeth flash in the darkness—a rare smile.

She smiled back, her mouth trembling a little. "Oh, Hauk…"

And then he dipped his head once more and took her nipple in his mouth.

Elli gasped and bowed her body up for him, offering herself, offering all she had to give as he caressed the aching bud, drawing on it, suckling her. She tossed her head against the pillow.

His hand strayed over her belly—and lower. He dipped a finger into the curls where her thighs joined. She cried out in excitement. Anticipation shimmered through her.

He raised his head from her breast and moved up a little, so his face loomed above hers. A blaze of lightning cut the night and she saw the feral gleam in his pale-blue eyes.

Thunder rolled and the room was dim again. Still, his eyes shone at her through the shadows. "I want to bring you pleasure, Elli."

"Oh, Hauk. You do. You *are*."

He brushed a kiss on her brow.

And below, very gently, he eased the curls aside, finding the slick groove of her sex. She gripped his big shoulders and whispered his name.

His finger moved. One long, shockingly intimate stroke and no more—right then. He took his touch elsewhere, sliding his rough and tender palm down the vulnerable inner surfaces of each of her thighs.

She sighed and let her legs ease open.

He was kissing her again. Kissing his way down the center of her. Elli lay beneath him, awash in pleasure, a willing victim of his mouth and his seeking tongue that dipped into her navel and played there. She gasped as she felt his teeth, lightly nipping. She moaned with the wonder of it—moaned and then moaned again.

Lower and lower, down over the tender skin below her navel. He put his lips there, against her mound, not delving in, just pressing his mouth, open, upon her.

And he let out a long, warm, focused breath of air.

Several bolts of lightning struck in quick succession, each followed by that rolling, booming sound. Elli was tossing her head on the pillow, muttering words she hardly knew the meaning of.

"Yes" and "Oh" and "Please" and "There…"

Gently, he moved her thighs wide apart and positioned himself between them. She dared to open her eyes, to gaze dreamily down the length of her own yearning body. His mouth was on her, now. And his tongue was...

His tongue was...

Elli groaned and the room lit up with wild stormy light. There was the thunder. And the hollow pounding, like a continuous sigh, of driving rain.

She clutched his golden head and she moved beneath his mouth and the soft explosion of fulfillment lifted her up, above the world, into the dark wet storm-shattered sky.

The only word she had was his name. And she said it. Over and over and over again.

For a while, they held each other and whispered and gently touched. It was a lovely time, a time for learning all the curves and hollows, all the tender places.

Each caress was a whisper. A question that found its answer in a sigh.

She traced the path of the lightning bolts—the one on his chest, the smaller, hidden one, in his palm. And the shape of the biggest dragon, the way its naughty tail curled down and down.

He said, "A wise woman never toys with the dragon...."

She closed her hand around him, so large and thick and wanting her. And she looked up into his eyes as she held him and the lightning blazed in the room.

He made a long, surrendering sound, a sound that

rolled low beneath the rumble of distant thunder. And he said her name, "Elli..."

And then she did for him what he'd done for her, first with long, slow strokes of her tongue and her hand and then more fully, her hair brushing his hard thighs, her mouth around him, drawing him into her, urging him on.

The hours went by in bursts of bright heat and shimmers of slow pleasure. More than once, she reached for the box on the bedside table.

Each time he caught her hand before her fingers could close on it. He took those empty fingers to his lips and he kissed them, one by one, drawing them slowly into his mouth, caressing them with his teeth and his tongue, then turning her hand over, laying his lips in the heart of her palm.

The third time he stopped her from reaching for the box, she took his hand and she kissed it chastely, then held it to her heart. "Why, Hauk? Why won't you let me—"

"Shh." He pulled her close.

He caressed her in long, slow strokes, running his hand down her back, over the twin curves of her hips and inward to find her wet and ready. Within minutes she was clutching him frantically, mindless with pleasure.

She didn't reach for the box again. She thought, as his wonderful hands and his talented mouth worked their magic on her hungry flesh, that it didn't matter, that maybe it was better this way—that she didn't have to be so greedy for everything all at once.

There would be time for them, together, for his body within hers. It seemed impossible to think it now—in some ways she felt she knew him better, even, than she knew her sisters—but she had to remember...

Four days ago, she hadn't even known he existed. Three days ago she'd found him, a total stranger, waiting in her apartment—to kidnap her—when she got home.

And here she was in a bed in a Boston hotel room, climbing all over him, thinking of words like *forever* and *I do*. Thinking of having his babies, of making a life with him.

Was that crazy or what?

He saw her dreamy smile and he asked her what had caused it.

She thought, *I think I love you,* but she didn't say it.

Like the box on the bedside table, the words of love could wait.

Some time after two, exhausted and deliciously satisfied, Elli dropped off to sleep in Hauk's arms.

When she woke, it was daylight. The storm had passed. The sky beyond the window across the room was cloudless. And she was alone in the bed.

She pushed back the covers, grabbed her pink shirt from where she'd thrown it on the floor and pulled it on over her head. Then, smiling the smile of a happy woman, she went to find him.

He hadn't gone far. She pushed open the door to the other room and there he was, fully dressed, sitting in a chair near the big window that took up half of one wall.

Out there beyond the glass, the harbor waters lay calm, the boats gently bobbing, a few of them, small pleasure craft, with sails as white as new snow. The orange ball of the rising sun lit up the clear blue sky.

Elli looked in his face and her happy smile faded. She knew that expression—that distant, composed look. She couldn't believe she was seeing it. She *refused* to believe she was seeing it.

"Hauk?" She ran to him—and then she drew herself up short. She wanted to reach for him. But somehow, she didn't quite dare. "Oh, Hauk, what's wrong? What's happened?"

His expression didn't change. "I have contacted the pilot. The plane is refueled and ready. Shower if you'd like, and get dressed. We need to be on our way."

Four days—going on five now—that she'd known him. Yet it felt like forever. It felt as if there had never been a time when Hauk FitzWyborn wasn't in her life. She knew him well enough to know that when he got that look, that tone to his voice, there was no reaching him, no hope that he might tell her what was going on inside him.

Still, she couldn't stop herself from trying. "I don't understand this." She spoke quietly. She wanted to be reasonable. She didn't want to start crying and begging and throwing herself on him, though that was exactly what she felt like doing. "What can have changed so much? Why are you so…far away? Last night, I thought that the two of us were—"

He put up a hand. She stared at the lightning bolt. Only hours ago, that hand had touched her in all her most secret places, giving her the kind of pleasure she'd never known before. And now he was using it to keep her at bay. "Last night was last night. It's over and done with."

"But I don't—"

"Enough." He stood. "Dress. Gather your belongings. I will take you to His Majesty, your father, where you belong."

She could feel anger rising, prickling the back of her neck, making her blood rush faster through her veins. "What are you saying, 'Where I belong'? I don't belong with my father. I don't even *know* my father. I'm going to visit him, and that's all. If I belong with anyone, I belong with—"

He put up his hand again. "Don't say it."

A furious shout rose in her throat. Somehow, she swallowed it and asked very quietly, "What have I done, for you to treat me like this?"

Something flashed in those pale eyes. It might have been pain. But he hid it quickly. Again, his face was stern and impassive. "Nothing. You have done nothing. Last night I was weak. And you were a beautiful, impossible dream I had—a dream that's over now. We won't speak of it again."

She whirled from him—she had to, to keep from flinging herself against him. She took two steps and then realized she had no idea where she was going. So she hovered there, with her back to him, not sure what to do next.

From where she stood she could see through the

open doorway to the tangled sheets of the bed where they'd spent last night. She could also see the night table, and the box that still waited, unopened, upon it. It all became pitifully clear to her, when she looked at that box.

She spun back to face him. "You *knew*." It was an accusation. "You knew last night that you'd do this in the morning. That's why you stopped me every time I tried to…" Her voice trailed off. There was no need to finish. The bleak look in his eyes said it all.

He confessed, so softly, "Yes. You understand. You have it right."

Oh, she saw it all so clearly. She *did* know him. They were worlds apart. He lived by codes and rules she couldn't begin to comprehend. Still, she knew him, knew how his mind worked, had seen down into his secret heart.

She whispered, "Because contraceptive devices are fallible."

"Yes."

"Because the only way to be certain conception won't happen is never to do what makes babies in the first place."

"That is correct."

"You are…saving yourself, aren't you? For the woman who will one day be your wife?"

"I wouldn't call it that."

"Then what *would* you call it?"

He gave a tiny shrug of those huge shoulders. "Protecting the rights of my children, making certain that when they're born, they're born legitimate. And protecting you, as well—protecting *your* children, who have the right to a father who's able to claim them.''

''So you'll only make love all the way with your wife.'' An absurd thought popped into her head—and she let it right out her mouth. ''Why, Hauk. You're a charter member of the NATWC.''

His brows drew together.

''NATWC,'' she said again, as if it was going to mean anything to him. ''The Never All the Way Club.''

Now, he looked completely confused. ''This is an American institution?''

She let out a wild laugh. ''Hardly.''

''Ah,'' he said uncomfortably. ''A joke. It's a joke.''

''Sort of. I guess.'' She felt foolish, to have even brought it up. ''It's just…something my sisters and I used to say to each other.''

''It makes no sense to me.''

''I know. Never mind. It doesn't matter. What matters is that there's no chance the woman you marry will ever be me. You won't let her be me. You won't let yourself even imagine the idea of a marriage to the daughter of your king.''

His mouth moved. She knew with absolute certainty he was about to say her name. But he didn't. He closed his lips over the word before it escaped him. And he started again. ''This is not about what I might imagine.''

''Then what is it about?''

''There can never be more between us. Accept it.

You are a princess and I am far beneath you. That's how it is. That's how it will always be.''

"But *why?* Why does it have to be that way? Why do you have to…limit yourself that way?"

"Questions," he muttered. "With you, the questions never end." He sounded weary. And strangely tender, too.

She stared at his mouth. She was thinking, *How can he be telling me it's over when it's hardly begun?*

How could anything so wrong be happening?

And where had her anger gone? It had left her, completely, just melted away. She missed it. Anger was so much better than this sad, empty feeling. "You should have told me last night—that it could never go anywhere, that last night was all we'd have."

"No. What I should have done was to send you away. But I didn't."

"And now everything's changed."

"Nothing is changed. I'll do what I have been ordered to do. I'll take you to your father."

"And then?"

"I'll ask for three weeks' leave."

Her throat closed up on her. She swallowed to make it relax. "Three weeks—that's how long I plan to visit."

"That's right."

It hurt, just to look at him and to know that if she reached out to him, he would step back. She stared past his shoulder, at the boats on the water with their white, white sails. But the sun was so bright.

She blinked and sun dogs danced at the corners of her eyes. "I feel...so much for you."

"You're young. What you feel will pass."

"Oh, please. That's a lame one and you know it. How old or young I am has nothing to do with how deeply I feel or how long it will last."

He stood so still and straight. She knew he was only waiting for her to give up this talk that he saw as pointless, to go and get dressed and get her things together so they could leave.

"I can't...reach you, Hauk. Not if you won't reach back."

"I can't reach back."

"That's not true."

"It *is* true. We're not the same, you and I. You see possibilities where I know there are none. We are what we are—and I am not the one for you."

"Only because you won't let yourself be. You won't give us a chance, won't even let yourself try."

"There's a line from an old Norse poem, *The length of my life and the day of my death were fated long ago.*"

"That may be. But it's what you'll *do* with your life, however long or short it may be, that we're talking about right now."

He chided gently, "Such a clever, clever tongue you have."

"I don't care what you say. You *can* reach back. You simply choose not to."

"All right. Have it your way. I choose not to."

Chapter Thirteen

It was early evening when they reached Gullandria, though the day, as yet, showed little sign of dimming. The flight attendant told Elli that at the summer equinox, which was a month and a half away, the sun would stay above the horizon for close to twenty hours, gradually fading into a long twilight.

"On a clear night in Gullandrian high summer," the attendant explained, "it never gets dark between sunset and sunrise."

They approached the island across the endless blue of the sea. At first, it all blurred together. Elli saw the rough shape of it, patches of green and black, puddles and fissures of deepest blue that were lakes and the major fjords. Then, as they got close, she had her first view of Lysgard, the capital, a harbor city low on the western shore, where the land curved sharply inward on its way to the southernmost tip.

As they flew in, Elli saw a jumble of steep-roofed compact houses that seemed to crowd each other on the fingers of land extending into the cobalt waters of the harbor. The close-packed dwellings clung to the green hillsides and perched above the steep black rock walls of Lysgard Fjord.

The attendant joined her at the window, pointing out the gold dome of the Grand Assembly, where freeman and jarl alike met to argue law and decide on matters of importance to the public at large. "The Grand Assembly is similar to the British Parliament, which, of course, owes its beginnings to the earliest assembly of its type—the Althing, where the Vikings of Iceland once gathered to make their laws."

She made special mention of the tall, proud spires of the largest churches. "Many think we worship the old Norse gods. But we say that we learn from them, that we take to heart what our earliest cultural myths have to show us. We in Gullandria are good Christians, of course—and look there." She pointed at the magnificent silver castle with its turrets and spires and glittering jewel-paned windows that crowned a jut of land above the city. Parkland like a green blanket fell away beneath it.

Elli found the sight enchanting. "It's like something from a fairy tale."

"Yes. Everyone says the same thing the first time they see His Majesty's largest palace. Isenhalla was built in the sixteenth century of rare silver Gullandrian slate. The slate has splendid reflective properties. It shines in the sunlight almost as if it were carved of ice.''

The urge came on Elli as it had several times during the flight, to turn in her chair, to ask Hauk some eager, touristy question. *So how's the fishing here? I understand it's always been one of the major industries.* Or *What about the oil refineries? Where are they? From what I've read, oil is the main export now....*

She did no such thing. Once or twice since they boarded, she'd dared to look at him. He'd stared back, unblinking, as if he were looking right through her. She'd felt like a naughty child at the gates of Buckingham Palace, trying to get one of those expressionless guards in a tall furry hat to crack a smile.

He was one hundred percent the king's warrior again. The man who had held her and kissed her and brought her to the heights of ecstasy the night before might never have been.

Her father wasn't there to welcome her when they touched down. He'd sent an entourage, though. She stepped off the plane and there they all were, including a color guard of ten proud soldiers in the red-and-black uniforms of the Gullandrian army. They carried the Gullandrian flag, which showed a red dragon coiled around a red tree on an ebony ground. The tree had thick, gnarled roots. Elli knew it represented Yggdrasill, the guardian tree of Norse mythology that anchored the cosmos, growing through all the nine worlds, from the underworlds up through Midgard, where men and giants walked, and on into the upper worlds of the gods and the light elves. There were other flags whipping in the wind, foremost among them the Thorson banner with its lightning bolt and hammer.

A small brass band played the national anthem and an aide stepped forward to read a long, flowery welcome speech from a device that rolled open like a modern-day version of a parchment scroll. Several yards away, a hundred or so Gullandrian citizens cheered and waved small flags, calling out, "Princess Elli, Princess Elli! Welcome! Welcome home!" There were reporters, too, and a news crew with the camera rolling. Guards kept them all behind a temporary barrier.

Elli played her part, waving and smiling and calling out, "Thank you! Oh, thank you!"

A limousine, more banners flying, rolled toward them. When it stopped, the aide who had read the welcome speech stepped forward and opened the door. With a final wave, Elli ducked inside.

The aide hustled in behind her. Elli looked back at the plane as they drove away, unable to stop herself from hoping for one last glimpse of Hauk. Maybe he'd be disembarking now she was safely in the car and on her way.

She saw the soldiers and the flags whipping in the wind and the people still cheering and waving. But no Hauk.

A black car with black-tinted windows rolled in behind them. Elli faced front and saw another car perhaps twenty feet ahead. Maybe Hauk was in one of them....

"May I say, Princess Elli, that it is an honor to escort you to the palace of His Majesty, your father." The aide, sitting down the long leather seat from her, was a tall, slender man in a dark, expensive-looking suit, attractive in a slightly fussy way.

"Thank you." He'd introduced himself a minute ago. And already she'd forgotten his name. She'd been thinking of Hauk, of last night, thinking that she couldn't believe it; that it couldn't be possible she would never see him again, never speak with him, never match her wits against his determination—and never, ever feel his kiss.

The aide looked at her hopefully. She put a little effort into recalling his name. Something beginning with prince. But then, in Gullandria, all the men's names started with prince—as long they were jarl and legitimate, anyway.

"It is only a short ride, under twenty kilometers, to Isenhalla," said Prince Whatever.

Elli gave the man a vague smile and looked out the window and wondered what Hauk might be doing now.

Three black Volvo sedans had been waiting at the edge of the airstrip when the royal jet landed. Two carried armed guards assigned to accompany the princess's limousine to the palace.

While Her Highness was busy listening to that endless welcome speech, Hauk had slipped off the plane and into the third car. Thus, at that moment he was on the way to the palace himself, well ahead of the royal limousine.

Perhaps the king would wish to speak with him today. Perhaps not.

If not, Hauk would busy himself in the stables. He was good with the stocky, white longhaired horses for which his country was famed, and he often helped with their training. But whatever he did—train horses or men, work up a sweat in the training yard himself, gamble with off-duty soldiers from the palace guard—until the king summoned him to hear his report, Hauk's real job would be to wait. When the king did send for him, he would make use of the audience to request leave.

Hauk sat in the back seat and stared out the window at the emerald-green fields and the karavik—hardy fat-tailed Gullandrian sheep—grazing on the slopes of the hills. To the north, the Black Mountains, gateway to the Vildelund, loomed tall and dark and capped with snow.

They were reaching the outskirts of Lysgard when Hauk's contact device, which he'd stuck in his boot for the flight, began vibrating. He asked the driver for a phone and placed the call to his king.

"Your Majesty. Hauk speaking. Her Highness, Princess Elli, is at this moment on her way to you."

"Yes, I know. She is well, in good spirits, from what my observers at the airport have told me."

"Yes, sire. She is well."

"I commend you, Hauk."

"I live only to serve, Your Majesty."

"I would have a word with you before I welcome my daughter in person. Come immediately to my private audience room."

* * *

When Hauk entered the royal chamber, King Osrik stood before the wide diamond-paned window. He stared out at the capital city below and the jewel-blue waters of the harbor beyond. It was 2100—nine in the evening American time—and outside the long twilight had begun. Also in the room, but in the corner near a bust of Odin, was a tall, gaunt figure with wise gray eyes, thinning white hair and a gray beard. He was the king's Grand Counselor, Prince Medwyn Greyfell. Prince Greyfell, who was second only to the king in power and influence, granted Hauk a small nod. In respectful response, Hauk put his fist to his heart and dipped his head.

The king turned from the window, knowing dark eyes warm with welcome. "Hauk. Hello." He held out the hand on which the ring of state gleamed.

In four strides, Hauk had crossed the big room. He swept to one knee and pressed his lips to the huge bloodred ruby that crowned the ring.

"Rise," said the king. "Sit with me." With a sweep of his hand, he gestured at two red velvet chairs with carved ebony arms, one on a small dais, the other placed lower, on the floor.

Hauk knew how to sit before his king, how to orchestrate the act of sitting, so that his liege always stayed slightly above him.

"There," said the king, once they had taken the chairs. He was smiling.

King Osrik had a good smile. It was open and confident, a smile that made people trust him. He was tall—not as tall as Hauk, but taller than most. His brows were dark and thick, his black hair streaked with silver. A handsome man, still strong and straight in his early fifties. Yes, there was sadness in those dark eyes sometimes. He had, after all, lost his greatest hope, his two sons. But he was a wise ruler and he knew that in front of his subjects, too much display of sadness spoke of weakness. And though a king no longer went a-Viking or carried a sword into battle as in days gone by, even in modern times, a king must never be thought weak.

"Tell me of my daughter," the king said, while from the corner the Grand Counselor listened and watched.

Hauk had a little speech prepared. "My lord, she is all a father could wish for in a daughter, all a king could wish for in a princess. Quick of mind and good at heart. Strong and beautiful. Raised American, of course. But she has studied the great myths. She has some background in our ways." Not as much as she *should* have, Hauk was thinking, though of course, he didn't say any such thing.

The king chuckled. "Quicker of mind than we had anticipated, I think."

Hauk dipped his head in acknowledgment of those words. "She drives a good bargain, sire."

"And with the queen, how did that go?" The king's smile had vanished.

"Her Majesty was…not pleased, that Her Highness would visit her father. But Her Highness held firm."

"She looked well?"

It took Hauk a moment to realize the king referred to his runaway queen. "Yes, sire. Very well."

The king insisted on hearing the details of the meeting with the queen. Hauk trotted them out, telling the story as briefly as possible, from the housekeeper's initial hostility, through the queen's distress at the news that the princess would travel to Gullandria, on to the calls to Princess Liv and Princess Brit, through the grim meal that he, the queen and the princess had shared, capping it all off with the queen's final acceptance of the inevitable.

"And it was Tuesday night, that my daughter went to the queen?"

"Yes, sire."

"She had that much more to do, in America, that she couldn't leave until the last minute we'd agreed on?"

"Sire, from my observation, after her visit with the queen on Tuesday night, all was in readiness for the princess to leave California."

"Yet she lingered there?"

"She insisted you had agreed she could stay in California until Thursday and she was not leaving until then."

"And what did you make of that—of her stalling?"

Hauk hesitated. He never felt comfortable when the king asked for interpretations of the motives of others. He always preferred to stick with the facts—especially now, when they were talking of the woman he had touched in ways that one such as he should never so much as dream of, when he felt certain that any moment he would betray himself as he had betrayed his king. That the king would sense the turmoil within him and want to know what was bothering him.

And that when the king began questioning him more pointedly, he'd answer bluntly, admit that he'd touched the king's daughter intimately, that all he longed for was to do it again.

He'd throw it all over—the life he'd built, all he'd worked so hard to earn, the bastard name he'd sought to make whole and proud. He'd throw it over because right now it all meant less than nothing to him. Right now it was empty as wheat chaff after threshing, of so little substance it was easily blown away by the wind.

Right now, he could almost open his mouth and confess what he'd done, redeem a shred of his tattered honor by taking whatever punishment the king saw fit to mete out.

But the thought of *her* kept him from that.

He couldn't say what it might cost her if her father learned where she'd spent the previous night. Perhaps little. Perhaps much.

At the very least, she would be shamed, diminished in her father's eyes. *That* he did care about. That made it imperative he keep the truth to himself.

The king sighed. "Ah, Hauk. Never mind." He spoke more briskly. "So. You left California yesterday morning, as agreed. And then a storm dragged you out of the sky and held you overnight in the city of Boston."

Hauk kept his eyes down and ordered the sudden, stunning erotic images out of his mind. "Yes, sire."

"But at last, here you are." The king rose, Hauk along with him. "Well done, my warrior."

Hauk stepped back and saluted. The interview was

almost over. He'd made it through without throwing his life away. The only thing left was to request leave.

The king spoke first. "A week from tomorrow is May Fair." There were three major fairs in the warm months: May Fair, Midsummer's Eve and Summer's End. "This year, in honor of my daughter, I'm planning a special celebration. War games and displays of horsemanship in the morning and afternoon. And along with the battle games and horse races, the usual festival, with music and poetry, games of chance and a bazaar. And then a feast. And then, at midnight, we'll set a ship ablaze in my daughter's honor.

"Notice has been sent out to all the fighting clubs." Gullandrian men liked to form fighting clubs. They would practice the old, wild ways of battle, and often stage fight shows at the local fairs. "As my warrior," said the king, "you will fight in my name."

There was only one response. "Your Majesty honors me."

"As you bring honor to our name. That is all, then."

Hauk hesitated again, unsure when he'd get another chance to ask for some time away from the palace. He was in a special position in regards to his orders. He took them only from the king.

The king gave him his opening. "You have more you wish to say, Hauk?"

"A request, Your Majesty."

"Name it."

"I'd like to take some leave, sire."

"When?"

"Right after I represent Your Majesty in the games next week."

"Is there some pressing reason you'll be going?"

He should have thought up a good story in advance. But he wasn't an effective liar, never had been. And lying always galled him, anyway. "No, my lord. I'd merely like some time to myself."

"No…personal difficulties?"

"None. Just holiday leave, my lord."

"Will a month do it?"

Three weeks, effective immediately, would have been better. That would have covered the entire length of time she planned to stay. But that wasn't possible. He must fight for his king.

And it should be all right. He felt reasonably certain he could avoid contact with her for the week to come. The king would keep her busy with tours and parties. And Hauk would stay near the stables and the training yard. It would all be so new to her. If she had a thought or two of him, she'd have no idea how to seek him out.

"I thank you, Majesty."

The huge ruby glittered as the king waved his hand. "Fight well for me. Then take your month and enjoy it. We have no crises brewing. There's a good chance your holiday will be uninterrupted."

Elli's limousine rolled into the huge paved court at the grand front entrance to her father's palace. The black escort cars kept going, down a side driveway and out of sight.

The aide led her up the wide steps, between the

intricately carved pillars, past the stone dragons and the statues of Odin and Freyja and Thor and turned her over to a phalanx of beautifully dressed young women who fisted their pretty hands to their designer-clad hearts and bowed their lovely heads.

One, a tall, graceful redhead with freckles across her patrician nose, stepped forward. "We are your ladies, Your Highness. I am Kaarin Karlsmon, first among those who will serve you." Kaarin was wearing a particularly fetching ensemble of midnight-blue silk with a pencil-thin skirt and a short, tight little jacket that showed off her trim figure. All the women wore beautiful jewels, to go with the gorgeous clothes.

Elli smiled and nodded and murmured hello over and over as each of the ladies introduced herself.

Finally, they led her inside, up a sweeping stone staircase and down a number of hallways to a set of wide carved doors. A pair of guards in red-and-black uniforms stood at attention, flanking the doors.

Elli's heart leaped in glad excitement. At last. She would meet her father.

But when the guards pulled the doors wide, she found herself looking through a marble-floored entrance area to a huge, beautifully decorated high-ceilinged drawing room—and no sign of the king, or anyone else for that matter.

"Your rooms, Your Highness," Lady Kaarin announced.

Elli was becoming a little tired of all the pomp and circumstance—not to mention the absence of the one person she'd come here to see. "Where's my father?"

Lady Kaarin smiled brightly. "He eagerly awaits you. But first, we are honored to make you comfortable, to see you bathed and suitably attired."

Elli thought, I'm clean and I'm ready. But she decided that announcing as much probably wouldn't sound very regal. She leaned close to the tall redhead and asked in a whisper, "I wonder...may I just call you Kaarin?"

"Certainly, Your—"

"And you'll call me Elli."

"Absolutely, Elli." Kaarin's soft mouth bloomed in a delighted smile.

"Kaarin, I must admit..."

"Anything, Your, er, Elli. Feel free to confide in me."

"Right now, I'd like a...reduction in my retinue. Say, just you. Could that be arranged?"

"Of course." Kaarin turned to the others. "Thank you all. The princess wishes her privacy now."

Dainty fists flew to chests, followed by a flurry of fawning farewells. And a minute later, Kaarin and Elli entered the spectacular drawing room alone.

Even Elli, who'd been raised in wealth and privilege, was impressed. The drawing room was big enough to use as a ballroom. More double doors led to a smaller sitting room. There was a fully equipped kitchen off the sitting room for any time she might have a sudden desire to whip herself up a little something to nosh on.

Kaarin laughed at that idea. "Of course you wouldn't, er, 'whip something up' yourself."

"I wouldn't?"

''A cook will be sent to you. And a chambermaid, of course. Cook and maid will be at your service at all times.''

There were two baths. The largest, off the bigger of the two bedrooms, included a whirlpool large enough to swim in and a sauna, double sinks and dual showers. Each room had huge fireplaces, with mantels of stone or dark wood intricately carved with dragons and Viking ships and scenes from the myths. The fireplaces all had beautiful inserts. Kaarin explained that they now burned gas. Gullandria was rich in oil, which meant that gas heat was more economical than burning wood or coal.

With a sweeping gesture, Kaarin indicated the whole huge suite. ''Will it do?''

''It's lovely. Now, when will I see my father?''

Elli's father, at that moment, was closeted with his Grand Counselor.

Beyond being his top advisor, Medwyn was also Osrik's closest—really his only—friend. The two had been bloodbound forty years before, when Osrik was a boy of twelve and Medwyn a bachelor and scholar of twenty-seven. At first, Medwyn had been Osrik's mentor and teacher. But time had made them equals. When the kingmaking had put Osrik on the throne, he'd risen above his friend.

Except when they were alone. To be bloodbound, after all, was to be closer than brothers, to share undying loyalty and support, each to the other. Osrik and Medwyn were bloodbound in the truest sense.

When Osrik was alone with his friend, all the formalities that set him apart as royalty could fall away.

The two were discussing Osrik's recent interview with the warrior.

"There seemed," remarked Medwyn thoughtfully, "something amiss with him. And much between the lines."

Osrik shrugged. "With Hauk, it always seems that way. The man is a true soldier. He'll never say two words where one will do. If we'd wanted conversation and clever analysis, we should have sent Finn Danelaw." Prince Danelaw was a notorious charmer—handsome and cunning, a master of intrigue. He owned a honeyed tongue and a tender manner no woman could resist. He bowed to no one but his king, to whom he was always unfailingly loyal.

Had they sent Finn to collect Elli, he would have had detail upon detail to share with them when he returned—what pleased Elli, what made her frown, what political positions she took—and what she yearned for in her most secret heart.

Also, Finn would have had a wealth of information about Ingrid....

But, no. There had been the possibility that Elli would have to be taken by force. Hauk was the best man for that.

And the choice of Danelaw would have presented one completely unacceptable risk.

Osrik said, "In the end, I still believe we were wise to decide against young Danelaw. He's *too* good with women. Elli most likely would have ended up in love with him—as all the women do. We'd have had a royal mess on our hands.''

Medwyn was nodding his white head. "The warrior has done the job assigned him. He's brought your chosen daughter safely home."

"I will get to know at least one of my lost girls at last." When he thought of that word, *lost,* Osrik felt sadness like a dark cloud pressing all around him.

A wife. Three daughters. One son and then the other. He had lost too much. It was time he took something back. "Eric?" he asked. "Still in the Vildelund?"

Like their fathers before them, Eric Greyfell and Valbrand Thorson had been bloodbound. Medwyn's son had been groomed all his life to walk in his father's shoes, to step up as Grand Counselor when the jarl declared Valbrand king. Both fathers had felt an inner peace that the future was as assured as any future could be.

All that was gone now.

Lost.

Eric—until then the most reasonable young man it had ever been Osrik's joy to know—had been crazed with grief at the disappearance of his friend. He'd insisted on striking off by sea to find out the truth of what had happened to Valbrand. He was determined to learn if vengeance was called for—and if so, to carry it out.

He'd returned a month ago having achieved little satisfaction in his quest. Everyone told the same story. There had been a storm and Valbrand was washed overboard. Eric could find no evidence of treachery.

Still grieving, still unsatisfied with the explanations of his friend's death, Eric had stopped only briefly to see his father, then headed straight for his family's village in the Vildelund—the wild country beyond the Black Mountains. Eric, like Valbrand, was much beloved by the people, but like his father, he owned a Mystic's heart. He found solace in the wild.

Medwyn was nodding. "I'll send for him, at your command."

"Give him time," said Osrik. "It would be better if he came on his own, better if it all happened... naturally. You know how young people are. Giving them orders only makes them determined *not* to do what's best for everyone."

"He's become something of a recluse since the tragedy last year. A command may be necessary to get him here."

"Still. We can wait awhile. And right now, I want to get to know this daughter of mine."

The two men regarded each other. There was no need to say more.

From all reports, Elli Thorson was a woman of integrity and strength. She was intelligent and beautiful, yet yielding, too. Not as driven and career-obsessed as her older sister, not as wild and contrary as the younger. Of Osrik's three daughters, Elli would make the best queen—especially, since, of the three, his spies had told him that Elli was the one who talked of marriage. Of children.

The fathers had it all planned. When Elli met Eric Greyfell, each would see the value in the other. Marriage would follow. When the time for the kingmaking came around again, Eric would be chosen.

And Elli would be his queen.

And if the gods smiled but for a moment on King Osrik Balderath Crosby Aesir Harald Einer Thorson, the day would come when his grandson would sit on the throne of Gullandria.

Chapter Fourteen

Kaarin insisted Elli take a long, hot bath. "And a sauna, too," Kaarin suggested. "There is nothing so effective at cleansing the body of toxins and impurities."

"Right. So does that mean you'd like a sauna yourself?"

"Your Highness, nothing would delight me more."

Before she saunaed with Kaarin, Elli called her mother. She got lucky and found Ingrid at home.

"Are you all right? You arrived safely?"

"Mom. I'm here. I'm fine. The palace is beautiful."

"Your father…?"

"I'll be seeing him soon. Call Brit and Liv, will you? Tell them I got here without a hitch and everything is all right."

"Nanna told me you left yesterday. I heard about that big storm on the east coast. Did you—"

"We had to land and wait it out in Boston." And it was the most perfect, incredible night of my life. "And now I'm here in Gullandria. Safe and sound."

"You'll call me, immediately, if you have a single...worry."

"Oh, Mom. Stop it. I'm fine and I'll *be* fine."

By the time Elli said goodbye to her mother, the chambermaid had appeared. She took charge of Elli and Kaarin's discarded clothes and offered huge white towels. Elli and Kaarin went into the wooden room together.

Ten minutes later Elli insisted she'd had enough. So they got out and stood under an icy shower spray, both of them shivering, Elli making whimpering sounds that had Kaarin giggling.

At last, Elli was allowed to climb into a scented bath and float for a while. That was nice. Soothing. Elli lay back and watched the steam trail up toward the arched stone ceiling and tried not to wonder what Hauk might be doing now.

After the bath came a real shower—in civilized warm water. Then Elli dried her hair and put on her usual light makeup. In the bedroom, the maid had laid out a hot pink number of lustrous silk that rivaled the one Kaarin wore. Elli put it on. It fit as if it had been made for her—which, she realized, it probably had.

"I think you are ready now to meet His Majesty." Kaarin was back in her blue silk and looking fantastic. She led the way.

It was a long walk, up one corridor and down another. At last, they turned a corner and came to another set of tall guarded doors.

"I'll leave you now," said Kaarin. "For this first meeting, your father wishes to see you alone."

Elli had hoped he would wish just that. "Thank you. For everything."

"It's my pleasure, Your Highness. I'll return in an hour. You'll find me waiting to escort you to your rooms when the visit is through." Kaarin set off down the hall and the guards opened the doors.

And there he was.

Her father.

So tall and handsome, in a beautifully cut designer suit, with eyes as kind as the voice she remembered from their phone conversation four days—and what seemed like a lifetime—before. The doors closed behind her and they were alone.

"Little Old Giant," he said.

The fond words did the trick. With a glad cry, Elli ran to him. He caught her in his arms and he held her close.

"I'm so glad you've come." He squeezed her tighter and rocked them both from side to side.

"Oh, Father. So am I."

Dinnertime had passed hours ago, but she'd had no chance to eat. In consideration of that, he'd had a simple meal laid out near one of the tall windows. They sat down across from each other.

Oh, he *was* kind. She could see it in his wise eyes, hear it in his gentle voice. Everything about him spoke of goodness. Now she'd finally met him, she couldn't comprehend why her mother had left him, what the deep, dark secret could be that had torn the two of them—and their family—apart.

As she looked at her father, Elli realized that in spite of everything—her mother's fears, her sister's warnings, in spite of losing Hauk when she'd barely managed to find him—she was glad she'd come.

Osrik asked her about her mother and her sisters and her life in Sacramento. She answered honestly and in detail and more than once had the feeling he already knew what she was telling him.

She supposed that didn't surprise her. Looking at him now, she knew in her heart that he'd never really given them up—not her, not her sisters. And not her mother, either.

He would have kept tabs on them over the years. And that didn't offend her in the least. He was her father, after all. Of course he'd want to know how his family was doing.

She longed to question him about Hauk—if he'd asked for leave, if he was gone on a new assignment now. But she also felt a definite reluctance to mention the warrior's name.

After all, Hauk was no fool. And he'd seemed so certain there was no hope for them, that what had happened between them should never have been.

Elli had trouble understanding why he felt that way, why he put himself beneath her and insisted that was where he had to stay. But then, she hadn't been brought up in Gullandria. As he was always telling her, she thought like an American.

She knew she had to be at least a little cautious. She needed to come up with some clever way to find out where he was now—and yet not reveal anything that might put him in a bad light with her father.

She set down her silver fork and picked up her water goblet. "Father, I have to tell you, I'm still a little upset with you."

Her father frowned. "But why?"

She drank and set the glass down on the snowy tablecloth. "For having me kidnapped. Where I come from, kidnapping is a crime."

He tried to slough it off. "What does it matter now? In the end, you decided you *wanted* to come."

"Yes, I did. But that doesn't make what *you* did acceptable."

Osrik's frown had turned to a scowl. "What's happening here? All of a sudden, you're lecturing me."

"I'm just trying to make you see that—"

He set down his own fork. "Elli, let me remind you. No one lectures the king."

"We're alone. No one's listening. I'd like to think, for now, we're just a daughter and her father, spending a little quality time together."

Her father reached across the table and patted her hand. "I like the sound of that. Let's not spoil it with an argument."

Elli kept pushing. "It was wrong, what you did. I was terrified at first."

He fell into her trap. "Did Hauk mistreat you?"

Elli ate a string bean, delicately, taking time to chew and swallow before answering. "Of course not. He was very gentle with me. And I know he only did what you ordered him to do." She had to watch it. Or she'd be smiling like a dreamy fool. Hauk, after all, had done a few things her father would never in a million years have ordered him to do.

"Well." Osrik's voice had turned gruff. "Forgive me then. And let's put what's done behind us."

Elli assumed an injured expression. "You should never have done that. You should never have—"

"We discussed this on the telephone four nights ago." Her father's voice was soft. And utterly unyielding. "There's no need to go into it again."

"No need for you, maybe."

"Elli," he said. Just her name and then dead silence. There was no kindness in those dark eyes now. He looked every inch the king. And the king was leaving this subject behind.

"This lamb is delicious," Elli said.

Her father's expression softened. "Yes. The meat of the karavik lamb is the most tender on earth. And the wool, as you've probably heard, is greatly prized. Our sheep, our horses, the fruits we pluck from the sea. These are the Gullandrian's pride."

"And your oil. Don't forget that."

"Our oil is our prosperity."

"I'll drink to that." She raised her wineglass. Her father raised his. They both drank. As she set her glass down again, Elli suggested, "You know, now you've got me thinking of him, it seems to me you ought to give Hauk FitzWyborn something." She was careful, to use his last name, to speak lightly, to keep the longing from her eyes.

Her father looked vaguely puzzled. "Give him something?"

"A reward. For a job well done. It wasn't exactly

a piece of cake getting me here. At first, I was absolutely determined not to come. I'd say, now I think about it, that it was kind of a minefield of an assignment, you know? To get me here no matter what—and to treat me like a princess while he did it.''

Her father cut another bite of lamb. "He's asked for leave. I've given it.''

Her heart sank. So. He was gone. Still, she spoke as if she hadn't a care in the world. "Leave? But wouldn't he get that anyway?''

Her father finished chewing and swallowed before he answered. "You may be right. I'll think about it. A week from tomorrow, he'll fight for us. He'll win. He always does. When I crown him the victor it's customary that he will claim a prize. Perhaps I'll grant him some attractive property—something with a few good buildings, with promising mineral rights and a large flock of karavik.''

Elli was stuck back there at the word *fight*. "Fight for us?''

Her father chuckled. "Next week is an annual celebration, May Fair. We always hold it in the parkland, below the palace grounds. This year, in your honor, we're adding a few extra events to the festivities.''

"Extra events that include fighting?''

"Picture a medieval fair. With battle reenactments and horse races—well, not precisely battle 'reenactments.' This will be more a battle *game*. Each man for himself, as it were.''

"I'm confused. I thought you said you'd given him leave.''

"Him?''

"Hauk. FitzWyborn."

"Ah. Yes, I did. But not till after the celebration. He's my warrior, after all. He fights in my name."

As soon as Osrik's daughter left the room, Medwyn slipped from his hiding place behind the heavy drape in back of the bust of Odin.

Osrik turned to his friend. "It went well, don't you think?"

Medwyn nodded. "She is lovely. Intelligence shines from her eyes."

"And good at heart, as well. You noted how she thought of FitzWyborn, how she was concerned that he receive his due?"

Medwyn didn't answer immediately.

Osrik chuckled. "I know that thoughtful look, old friend. Speak up. What's bothering you?"

But Medwyn only waved a long, pale hand. "It's nothing, nothing at all. My son is a lucky man."

The heavy curtains were drawn at all the windows, making it as dark as it would have been at home, where the sun set and true night followed.

But Elli couldn't sleep.

She couldn't stop thinking of Hauk. She missed him terribly. And the idea that she'd see him only once more, from a formal distance, while he did whatever he did when he fought in her father's name...

Well, she wouldn't accept that.

It wasn't right. It hurt too much.

Something had to be done.

But then again, what if she'd read him all wrong?

What if he didn't feel for her as strongly as she felt for him? Maybe even if he *could* give himself permission to love her, he wouldn't. Maybe she simply wasn't the woman for him.

That *was* possible. Though in her soul, she didn't believe it.

But it could be the truth. It might have to be faced—and to do that, to face that, she had to *see* him, to *speak* with him.

She just couldn't stop hope from springing up inside her, from whispering in her ear that there had to be a way.

And for more than just a private moment.

A way for the two of them. A way that they could be together—proudly. And openly. If he only wanted that, *yearned* for that, as she did.

Damn it, this was the twenty-first century. The woman tenth in line to the British throne claimed no title, had a stud in her tongue and had lived openly with a commoner boyfriend. And that was a good thing, the way Elli saw it. A woman ought to be able to live her life without everyone around her bowing and scraping and calling her "Princess." A woman ought to be allowed to follow her heart. And no honest man should have to turn away from a woman he could love simply because some cruel cultural stigma declared him beneath her.

That morning, in Boston, Hauk had taken her totally off guard. She'd been too stunned and hurt to muster her best arguments. He owed her another chance to state the case for love.

And Elli Thorson intended to see to it that she got what he owed her.

She spent the sleepless night making plans.

First of all, she needed to get in touch with him. And she didn't have a clue where to go to look for him. She considered confiding in Kaarin, asking her if she knew where the king's warrior might be found.

But on second thought...

Kaarin seemed nice enough, but she was so clearly an aristocrat, a little bit formal, very aware of her place. Elli's instinct was that it would be unwise to share secrets with her. And at this point, really, all she had were her instincts.

Maybe she could befriend the chambermaid or her cook. Elli had no doubt both of them would have the information she sought—or would know where to get it.

Elli had grown up with servants around her. Besides Hildy, who was really like one of the family, there were always a couple of maids and often a chauffeur living in the apartments over the garages at the house in Land Park.

"Never underestimate the knowledge of your servants, girls," her mother had told her and her sisters when they were only children. "They know everything about you. They know all the secrets you don't want to admit they've learned. Treat them with respect and fairness always, and as a rule they'll repay you with loyalty and hard work. Treat them shabbily and they will sell your secrets and never think twice about it."

But to befriend the servants would take time. She

only had a week. She would have to watch and listen—see if she got a sense that either the cook or the maid might be someone who would help her get to Hauk.

Oh, this was all so...difficult. Was she making too much of it? Should she simply do what she'd do if she were home in Sacramento? Ask anyone who might have information—Kaarin, her father, the chambermaid, the cook? And take it from there.

Her instincts kicked in again. And they told her no. They told her to proceed with caution.

For two days, Elli learned nothing about where to find Hauk. She thought she would go stark, raving head-banging nuts—longing only for a word with him, and getting instead formal audiences with her father and numerous princes and well-born ladies, enduring extended tours of the Grand Assembly chambers and the harbor area, of a farm outside the city and a huge, hangarlike workshop where talented craftsmen still built the sleek, narrow Viking-style ships for pleasure use and for racing.

And feasts. They had huge dinners both nights, followed one night by music and dancing and the other by long renditions of a couple of the lesser-known Norse myths as recited by a leading poet/minstrel, or *skald*.

The night they had dancing, she was led out onto the floor by a number of handsome princes. One she thought especially good-looking—and probably a danger to any girl whose heart wasn't already otherwise engaged. Finn Danelaw was his name. She would have enjoyed flirting with him if she were capable of flirting with anyone right then. In fact, she could almost have been angry with Hauk for that, for stealing away her pleasure in the company and conversation of other men.

Finally, Sunday night, as she lay in bed, awake as usual, doubting she would ever speak to Hauk again, she figured out how to find him. It was so simple, she couldn't believe she hadn't thought of it earlier.

Monday morning, she requested an extensive tour of Isenhalla and the grounds and parkland surrounding it. Her father thought it was an excellent idea. He had matters of state to attend to, however, and couldn't take her around himself. He assigned the job to the prince who'd met her at the airport.

She and Prince What's-it spent the morning and early afternoon inside the palace, touring the endless, echoing rooms. Elli expressed fascination with all of it—the precious antiques, the Austrian crystal chandeliers, the huge tapestries in the formal audience hall that had come from France and were over five hundred years old.

The prince finally led her outside. They wandered through the formal gardens. She admired the tennis courts and the green swathe of velvet-textured grass where the courtiers played croquet.

Her heart knocking harder in hope and anticipation, she asked to see where the soldiers of the palace lived when off duty. Though Prince Whoever-he-was clearly didn't approve, he took her to the long, high-roofed barracks. He even allowed her a quick look at the yard and the enormous, fully equipped gymnasium where the men trained.

Elli saw a lot of soldiers. But not the one she sought.

Next they went to the stables so she could have a look at the famed longhaired white Gullandrian horses.

And there he was.

In a round pen, working with a young and spirited mare.

Elli's pulse went racing and her whole body felt suddenly light as a sunbeam. She balanced on air.

She turned a blinding smile on Prince What's-his-name. "There's Hauk FitzWyborn. My escort here, to Gullandria. I have to say hello."

"Uh," said the prince, for once at a loss for words. "Oh, well. Of course, Your Highness. Whatever you—"

She didn't hear the rest. She had eyes and ears for one man only and that man stood in the center of the pen, working a long lead, guiding the plucky mare to prance in a circle and toss her snowy head, her long mane and silky coat streaming in the breeze.

He saw her as he guided the horse around to where she stood. He never paused in working that lead, in coaxing the horse on in a circle. But for a split second, his gaze met hers.

The world was in that second. The universe in that shared look.

She knew then with absolute certainty that the problem was not that he didn't want her.

The prince came and stood beside her. She stared

at Hauk, smiling. Waiting. Absolutely calm—at least on the surface. Inside she was all quivers and needles and pins.

In the end, he had no choice but to lead the mare from the pen and hand her off to a groom. He came toward them, so stunningly male all the breath flew right out of Elli's body and every last drop of saliva dried up in her mouth.

"Your Highness," he said, removing his rawhide gloves, then bringing his big fist to his chest and dipping his gold head. "Prince Onund."

Elli swallowed to moisten her bone-dry mouth and resisted the urge to remind Hauk playfully that she'd given him an order a week ago and she expected him to obey it. He was never to call her Your Highness again.

But his beautiful light eyes had warnings in them. *Say nothing too casual, betray nothing of what has been.* She heard them as if he spoke them aloud.

"Hauk. Good to see you." She held out her hand. He had no choice but to take it. She saw his eyes narrow—just a fraction—when he felt the tiny folded square of paper she passed him. But his face, as always, remained carefully controlled. He bowed over her hand and released it. Her skin flamed where his had touched it.

She granted him a cool smile. "I hope you are well."

"My health, Princess, is excellent."

Princess. Your Highness. She could see that gleam in his eyes. He was *enjoying* the opportunity to disobey her command.

Prince Onund spoke up, putting clear emphasis on the first syllable of Hauk's name. "*Fitz*Wyborn works frequently with the horses. He seems most comfortable in the company of livestock."

Elli had learned a few things at her mother's knee. One was how to deliver *the look. The look* was designed to put upstarts in their place. *The look* clearly said, *If you don't watch it, you'll never do lunch in this town again.*

She turned *the look* on the prince. That shut him up. She turned back to Hauk. "I guess I never mentioned while you were…making sure I arrived here safely, that I love to ride."

Okay, it was a serious exaggeration. She'd never be the horsewoman her sisters were—Liv because she had to do everything well, Brit because riding a horse, like flying a plane or mountain biking, came as naturally to her as breathing. But Elli *had* ridden. Aunt Nanna kept horses at her vineyard in Napa. All three girls had learned to ride as children. "I think, tomorrow, I'll go riding. I'm sure I can dig up some suitable clothes." There were clothes for days in the huge closets in her dressing room. It only made sense that riding gear would be among them. "Since you're the expert around here when it comes to horses, I'd like you to ride with me, Hauk. Would you mind?"

He looked at her coolly. Distantly. She wondered if she had it all wrong after all, if he really wanted nothing to do with her—if he'd felt only relief once he got her off his hands last week.

But then he said what he had to say. "I would be honored, Your Highness."

"Thank you. In the morning, I think. Early. That way I won't disrupt whatever schedule my father has planned for me. Say, eight? I'll meet you right here."

"As you wish, Princess."

"Great." She turned to the prince. "Well, Onund. Why don't we go on in and have a look at the stables?"

The prince's worried expression brightened considerably. "Certainly, Your Highness."

"And then maybe we could check out the progress they're making on the preparations for Saturday's big celebration."

"Absolutely." The prince offered his arm. Elli took it. "This way," he said.

They turned for the stables.

Hauk put his fist to his chest and lowered his head. He didn't look up until the prince had led the princess through the open stable door. Then he stuck his fist in his pocket, letting go of the small square of paper she had passed him.

He wasn't going to take it out. Ever. He would forget it was in there. To him, it would be as if it didn't exist.

Hah.

And while he was at it, he'd forget to draw his next breath.

He lasted less than an hour. Then he flung himself down under a birch tree out in the horse paddock, near the clear, narrow creek. There was no one nearby. A gelding and a pretty mare nibbled grass over by the fence. They weren't the least interested that the king's warrior had lost so completely what he once prized most: his self-control.

Hauk shut his eyes and leaned his head back against the tree trunk—hard. The impact should have knocked some sense into him. But it was no good.

His blood whispered her name as it ran through his veins—her true name, her given name: *Elli, Elli, Elli, Elli...*

His hands shaking like those of a palsied man, he took out the little bit of paper and spread it open on his thigh.

It read, *Meet me. Here. Tonight at midnight.*

Chapter Fifteen

As far as Elli was concerned, there were way too many hours to live through until midnight. Every one of them seemed to take a lifetime to go by.

At eight that evening, she and her father had dinner again in the private audience room where she'd met him that first night. She was glad for some time alone with him. She had questions she needed to ask—about her lost brothers, about whether he thought their deaths were really accidental.

Her father answered thoughtfully. "There's always the possibility that treachery was involved. In both cases. But our best people looked into Kylan's death—police and the NIB."

"NIB?"

"National Investigative Bureau—similar to your FBI in America. They found no evidence that the fire was set. And all our reports about Valbrand are the same. No foul play. There was a storm. He didn't survive it.''

He spoke with sad conviction. Elli found she believed him—or at least, she believed that *he* believed what he told her. If either of her brothers had been murdered, she was certain her father didn't think so. Osrik must have insisted that the investigations be thorough. And he honestly seemed satisfied that they'd turned up nothing suspicious because there was nothing suspicious to find.

He'd spoken so frankly of her brothers, she dared to ask the other question that had troubled her all her life—the question her mother would never answer.

''What happened, between you and Mom? What made her take me and my sisters and leave here forever?''

He looked away. ''Your mother will have to answer that one.''

That was all he would say—the same thing her aunts always said. Elli found herself wondering if she'd ever learn what had ripped her family apart all those years ago.

At a little after ten, she left her father to return to her rooms. She walked back alone. As she'd become more accustomed to the layout of the palace, she'd been allowed to find her way around on her own now and then.

Of course, when she got to her suite, the two guards were waiting. She was reasonably certain they'd have reported to her father if she hadn't shown up, that they'd be reporting to her father if she left again. She doubted there was much Osrik would do with that knowledge—unless he heard she'd gone somewhere he didn't approve of.

Like maybe out to the stables to get it on with a guy whose name began with Fitz.

Elli was beginning to see now that the fitz thing was a big problem. She'd heard it more than once—in the way that jerk Onund had said *Fitz*Wyborn, in any number of casual, cutting remarks. "Hopeless as a fitz," was a favored Gullandrian pejorative. "Bastard son of a fitz," was another—meaning that one's father (or mother) hadn't learned his lesson by being born in shame, but had gone ahead and produced a few fitzes of his own. And "fitzhead." Now, there was a colorful one.

It all seemed utterly ridiculous to Elli. But it must have been terrible for Hauk, growing up. The constant abuse had to be killing.

It was a miracle he'd turned out as he had, honorable to the core. So very strong. And good.

The guards opened the doors for her and she entered her rooms. The chambermaid was waiting. Elli thanked her and told her she wouldn't need her until seven the next morning. The girl smiled slyly, dropped a curtsy and left. There was a boyfriend. Elli had seen them, in the shadows on the back stairs, sharing kisses. Elli was glad her maid had found a special guy. It was one less pair of prying eyes to worry about when midnight came.

Elli's cook, who had a real fondness for schnapps, would already have retired to her room with her bottle. No worries there.

Elli went looking for her own clothes, the ones she had brought from home. After a ten-minute search, she found what she needed, a pair of jeans, a dark T-shirt and her trusty comfy sneakers. She pulled her hair back into a ponytail and put on the blue visor she always took with her on trips—not because it would be bright outside, but because maybe, if someone happened to see her, they wouldn't guess who she was.

She had the way scoped out: down the back stairs. The stairs led to a long, narrow hall on the ground floor. At the end of that hall, there was a servants' entrance. From there, it wasn't that far to the stables.

Elli found it kind of funny that her father would take such care to place guards at her door—and then leave the back stairs unattended. But then, as far as he knew, she had no reason to sneak around at night. And maybe the cook and maid were supposed to keep an eye on her. Who could say? Maybe the guards were only for her protection—or their presence was simply part of palace protocol. It didn't matter. No one would see her leave if she could help it.

At eleven-forty, she slipped out the door in the kitchen. She met no one on the dim, narrow stairs. A guard patrolled the area outside the back door. But luck was with her. His back was to her. She slipped across the short space of grass and into the cover of the trees.

A gap in the garden hedge was her gateway into open parkland. She ran across the damp grass that shimmered in the faint glow of deepest twilight. She reached the stables and the training pens within minutes and ducked quickly into the shadows cast by one of the long, steep-roofed buildings.

From there, she had an unobstructed view of the round pen where she'd found Hauk training the high-stepping mare that morning. He wasn't there.

She took off her visor and smoothed her hair. It was still a few minutes till midnight. Maybe—

Right then, a big hand closed around her mouth. She was yanked back against a hard chest.

She knew instantly who held her—knew the feel of him, the scent of him. He took his hand from her mouth and turned her to face him.

"Oh, Hauk…"

He gestured for silence and grabbed her hand.

She followed him willingly, a silly grin on her face, around the end of the building and through the open door into the stable. From a few of the stalls she heard soft whickering sounds. He pulled her on, between the rows of stalls to a door at the back. They went through it. He shut the door behind them and flicked a switch on the wall. A bare low-wattage bulb suspended from the rafters popped on.

It was a tack room, windowless, with straw on the floor and bits and bridles hanging on pegs. There were rows of saddles and shelves stacked with blankets.

He led her over to a long, rough pine bench. "Sit down."

She obeyed him, dropping her visor next to her and folding her eager hands in her lap so that they wouldn't get too bold and start grabbing for him.

He loomed above her, looking down, his expression depressingly grave. "You shouldn't be here. This is wrong."

"Lovely to see you, too."

"I told you there could be nothing more, ever, between us. I told you—"

"I don't want to hear it."

"You're a fool and I'm—"

"—here," she finished for him. "You're here. You came."

"Because I—"

"Oh, don't say it. Don't tell me any lies. We both know why you're here and it's nothing to do with my wish being your command."

"There can be no more between us."

"Oh, stop," she hissed in an impassioned whisper. "Stop right now." She shot to her feet and he backed up a step. "You'll never convince me you mean that—and if you believed it yourself you wouldn't have to keep saying it over and over and over again."

"Keep your voice down."

"All right, fine," she whispered. "My voice is down. But I will talk. I will say what I came here to say."

"Oh, you'll talk," he muttered. "I know you will. You'll use that clever tongue of yours until you have me convinced that black is white and up is down."

That hurt, for some reason. She dropped back to the bench. Gripping the edges of it, she looked down at the straw beneath her sneakers. "I just…I want tell you. I *have* to tell you." She looked up, into those eyes she wanted to look in for the rest of her life. "I love you, Hauk. I'm *in* love with you."

He blinked. His face went utterly blank—a stunned kind of blank, the way a man would probably look right after an enemy shoved a knife between his ribs.

Her heart was breaking. "Oh, please. Don't look at me like that. It can't be as bad as that."

"Elli..."

Her name. *Her first name.* He had said it. He had said as if it was all he ever thought about.

Joy leaped like a hungry flame within her. She gripped the bench harder. It seemed very important not to fling herself at him, not to force an embrace when he wasn't ready for one.

"I love it when you say my name," she whispered. "You do it so seldom."

"It's not appropriate."

She couldn't keep from scoffing. "As if I care. As if that matters in the least. As if what's appropriate has a damn thing to do with—" She cut herself off. To rant at him was not the way. She sucked in a calming breath and she tried again. "Hauk. Listen. Could you...do you think it might be possible that you could love me back?"

"What I feel means nothing."

She felt her anger rising. She put all her will into keeping it down. "What are you talking about? What you feel is half of it—half of what we need, to start building something, together, you and me." She swallowed hard and she lifted her head high and she told him what she wanted. "Hauk. I know I'm rushing this, but you've boxed me into a corner here. There's no other way but to tell you now, to...say it all, now. This may be my only chance."

He started to speak.

"Please," she said.

He gave her a tight nod.

And she told him. "I want us to be married. I know what this is, between you and me. I know you're the man I've been looking for. I want *you*. I want to be the woman you finally make love with all the way. Because I want to be your wife. I want my babies to be *your* babies. I'll…take your name proudly. As our children will. Please. Won't you just consider it?"

For a moment, in his eyes, she saw that he wanted exactly what she wanted.

And then he denied her again. "You don't understand. You refuse to see. Some things are never done."

"You mean, because you're illegitimate?"

"A fitz can only be allowed to reach so high."

"You're saying it's *never* happened? No one like you has *ever* loved someone like me?"

"Certainly it's happened. And those lovers either gave each other up. Or it ended badly. In mutual bitterness. Or worse. Men—and women—who reach too high tend to die in mysterious ways."

"I won't believe that. My father would never—"

"Elli." His voice was so tender. All the love he wouldn't declare was there in it. "I didn't say the king would have me killed. I don't believe that either." For a split second, his eyes shifted away and she wondered if maybe he *did* believe exactly that. And then he was looking straight at her again. "I don't know what would happen to me. I doubt, other than the shame of dragging you down, that it would be anything I wouldn't survive. But I know, unequivocally, that you would be disgraced to stoop so low."

She jumped to her feet again. "No. No, you don't know that." She drew herself up. "All this…*fitz* thing, it's nothing to me. If people look down on me for loving you, then those are people whose opinions I don't give a damn about. Oh, Hauk. Maybe I don't get it. Maybe I don't understand how really powerful this thing is, this judgment of a person by what his parents did. Maybe I'm asking for disaster. But then again, maybe you underrate yourself. Maybe you've been trained since childhood to see yourself as so much less than you are. Maybe if we went to my father, together—"

He didn't even let her finish. "No. It's no good. I want you to go back, now. To your father's house. Tomorrow, when you come to ride, someone else will be assigned to ride with you. You won't see me. Please don't ask for me. Don't look for me anymore."

She stared at him. It seemed impossible that he was doing this—sending her away like this. Forever.

She couldn't stop herself. She tried one more time. "Just…think about what I said. Think about it. That's all. Because deep in your heart, you have to know that love is never wrong. If you never…come to me, I truly hope that someday you'll find someone. That you'll love her as you won't let yourself love me. That your life will be a good life, a happy one. A full one.

"And for myself, I hope the same thing. That I'll get over you. Find someone else. Make myself the kind of life I've always wanted, with a good man.

And our children. But that isn't going to happen for a long time. So if you change your mind—''

"I won't."

She felt the tears gathering. She swiped them away and turned briefly to grab the visor she'd left on the bench. It took her a minute to collect herself, a minute in which she fought, as she'd fought since he'd brought her into that windowless room, to keep from throwing herself on him, to keep from crying like a baby, begging him to give her—and all they might share—some kind of a chance.

Finally, when she thought she could speak without bursting into tears, she said quietly, "I'm just telling you. I'm here. I'm ready. If you dare to reach for me, I'll be reaching back. I won't disappoint you. I'll never let you down."

Chapter Sixteen

Hauk stood by his word. The next day, when Elli went out to ride, a captain of the guard was waiting for her. She smiled and greeted the man politely and mounted the sweet-natured gelding he'd already saddled before she got there. By ten, she was back in her rooms. She showered and changed and then went down into the city with Kaarin and a few of her other ladies. They shopped. They did lunch.

The days went by in a whirl of tours and endless state dinners with dancing afterward. Elli tried to smile through it all, to forget about Hauk and enjoy her visit to her father's land. It wasn't easy. But most of the time she thought she managed pretty well.

She and Osrik shared a third private meal on Friday night. He asked her if she was troubled. He said he'd noticed that sometimes she seemed a little sad.

Elli lied. She told him there was nothing important, that it was all pretty overwhelming, being here, being pampered and photographed and constantly in the limelight. But really, she was having a wonderful time.

After dinner, Kaarin joined her in her rooms to give her a few instructions about the part she would play in the various ceremonies at May Fair the next day. Kaarin left around eleven.

Elli dismissed the maid and went to bed. She slept well, for once. She woke in the morning feeling surprisingly rested, thinking that over time, she would be all right.

Today would be rough. She'd have to see Hauk again—probably give him the victor's token if he won in the mock-battle as her father seemed certain he would.

But once she got through that, it would truly be over. He'd be gone. She wouldn't have to wait and wonder if maybe he'd change his mind and come to her. Or if maybe she'd just happen to run into him somewhere and have to exercise all her self-control to keep from saying or doing something they'd both regret.

When he returned from his leave, she'd be home in California. Slowly, over time, she'd get used to the idea that she'd loved him and he couldn't let himself love her in return. Her heart would heal.

Over time.

By one in the afternoon, Elli had been introduced to more prosperous freeman merchants than she cared to count. She'd been photographed with her father and her ladies, with various adoring princes and a phalanx of elected officials called assemblymen, who were roughly equivalent to congressmen in America.

It was a beautiful day, breezy and cool in the morning, slightly warmer now the afternoon had come. The parkland was lush with spring green, the leaves of the aspen trees quivering sweetly in the slight sea-scented wind. The sky overhead was cloudless, a clear, cool blue.

Like Hauk's eyes, she couldn't help thinking, though she knew that such thoughts did her no good at all.

"Princess Elli, Princess Elli! Best oatcakes in Gullandria," called a merchant from a nearby booth. Elli led her chattering ladies over there. She took a bite of the offered oatcake, chewed, swallowed and announced, "Outstanding." Though of course, she wasn't really any kind of judge of a good oatcake.

"Princess Elli! This way!"

Obediently, Elli turned to the cameraman, making certain the proud merchant would be in the shot with her.

"Have another bite!" shouted the cameraman. Elli bit into the oatcake as the merchant beamed with pleasure and the cameraman got his shot.

An hour or so later, when Kaarin whispered that it was time to meet His Majesty again in the royal box at the edge of the area designated as the battlefield, Elli was glad to go.

Though her chest felt tight and her stomach unsettled at the prospect of seeing Hauk for the last time, it was a relief to escape the endless photo-op for a minute or two. The past week in Gullandria had brought her a true understanding of the ambivalence of public figures toward the press. They could suck a person dry with their cameras and their shouting and their constant demands.

She climbed the steps to the high box and took the seat next to her father. He smiled on her fondly, caught her hand and brought it to his lips. The rows of people across the open field from them and in the stands around them cheered at the sight.

The fight was nothing like she'd expected it to be. It was absolutely wild, with no order or discipline that Elli could see. The men poured onto the field at a run and then turned without ceremony and began hacking away at each other. Elli watched with her heart in her throat.

Battle garb included leggings and soft boots. Some wore light chain mail, "Called a *byrnie*," Kaarin, who sat behind her, whispered in her ear. "Or Odin's shirt, or a battle-cloak..." Some wore rough shirts that ended above the knee and were belted at the waist. Some wore breeches belted with a sash—and nothing above the waist. "The king's berserkers," Kaarin told her with pride. "They fight bare-chested."

Hauk was one of those. The sight of him stopped Elli's heart dead in her chest—and then sent it racing triple-time.

Kaarin said, in a throaty, excited whisper, "He's magnificent, isn't he? The king's warrior? Too bad he's a fitz.'' Elli felt her blood rising. It took all the self-control she possessed not to turn in her seat and inform the Lady Kaarin that Hauk was the finest man she knew and this whole narrow-minded prejudice against people who'd had the misfortune to be born to unmarried parents made her sick to her stomach.

If she could be certain that was all she would say, she might have done it. But her emotions rode a razor's edge right then. She might say anything. She might blurt out that she loved him. For herself, that wouldn't matter. She'd be proud to announce her love to the world.

But she hadn't forgotten the way Hauk's gaze had slid away the other night, when he'd said he didn't believe her father would harm him if he knew what they felt for each other. There seemed no reason, since what they felt for each other wasn't going anywhere, to put her father to the test.

Somehow, she stayed facing front—and luckily, she didn't have to look composed.

Nobody did. The spectators shouted and stomped and called out coarse encouragements.

Weapons were axes and spears and heavy double-edged swords. Each man carried a brightly painted round shield. Along with all the shouts from the stands, the men on the field yelled and cursed and let out wild, mad-sounding shrieks. Add to all that the clanking and thudding of weapons—blade to blade, ax to shield.

Blood flowed—but not *too* much of it. Elli kept telling herself it was all just a show.

But then, near the center of the melee, the first man

went down. He shouted in pain, dropped, sprawled—and lay still.

Elli let out a sharp cry of dismay.

Her father patted her hand. "They train fiercely to make it a good show. Watch closely. When a weapon touches a man at a vital spot, he has to go down."

"You mean he's not dead?" Another man fell, right then. Elli stood and peered closer. Then she dropped to her chair again. "You're right. I think he's breathing."

Her father chuckled. "My daughter, in this battle, all the dead still breathe."

One by one, the men fell. When a man went to the ground, he stayed there, unmoving, until the field was littered with the breathing "dead."

The spectators quieted as the fight wore on. And fewer men fighting meant the blows seemed to ring out louder, the individual battle cries seemed all the more powerful, all the more fraught with deadly intent.

Hauk fought on. Elli couldn't take her eyes from him. He was so beautiful, the dragon rearing, the lightning bolt striking, laying low all who dared to challenge the sharpness of his sword. The powerful muscles of his arms and back gathered and flexed with each blow. He'd been cut, here and there, and his body ran sweat. His smooth skin gleamed in the sunlight, streaked with red.

In the end, as her father had predicted, all the men had dropped to the field save one. And that one was Hauk.

He stood in the center of the wide grassy space

now littered with the fallen and he turned in a slow circle, raising sword and shield as he moved.

The crowd went wild, screaming, "The king's champion! The king's warrior! The victor!"

The wild shouts faded. Someone started clapping. Within seconds, the others joined in, clapping in a steady rhythm.

One loud voice shouted above the clapping, "Hauk!" And the name became a chant. "Hauk, Hauk, Hauk, Hauk!"

Hauk made a full circle until once again he faced the royal box. He lowered his weapon, his shield— and his head. The chant from the people died, the clapping stopped.

And a stream of young barefooted women dressed in gauzy white gowns ran onto the field. Each knelt by a fallen warrior and helped him to his feet.

"To Valhalla," shouted the spectators. "To Valhalla and the glorious feast!"

The young women, Elli knew, represented the Valkyries, the battle maidens who took the honored dead from the battlefield and led them to Odin's great hall, there to feast and fight for eternity.

The white-gowned girls led the slain warriors away. Hauk was left alone on the field, sword and shield lowered, head bowed.

Elli knew what to do. Kaarin had drilled her the night before. She slid a hand into her pocket and her fingers closed around the king's token—a silver charm of Thor's hammer on a heavy silver chain. She watched her father and stood when he did.

Her heart was rising, too. Oh, it really did feel as if it had lodged in her throat.

The crowd fell silent.

Her father called out in sonorous tones, "Come forward, my warrior!"

In long, proud strides, Hauk came toward them. When he reached the royal box, he dropped to one knee.

"Rise, warrior," her father said, as Kaarin had told Elli he would.

Hauk stood. For a split second, his eyes met hers. Elli felt the contact like a blow to her soul. But then instantly, his gaze shifted. He faced her father.

She felt bereft, empty. It was just like the other night, in the tack room at the back of the stable. She wanted to burst into tears.

Of course, she did no such thing. She was made of sterner stuff than that.

Her father spoke again. "You bring our daughter home to us. And here, today, you bring honor to our name in the game of battle. It is your right to claim a prize. What will you have?"

Hauk was to say what Kaarin had told her the victor in the games always said at that moment, *Whatever my king will grant me.* And then her father would name the prize and Elli would present the token.

But Hauk didn't say what the victor always said. He faced his king proudly and he said out loud and clear, "I would have Princess Elli to be my wife."

You could have heard an aspen leaf whisper its way to the ground. Every man, woman and child in the stands and in the boxes sat stock-still, gaping. No one believed the warrior could possibly have said what they had all heard him say.

Elli was aware of the huge hole of silence. But only vaguely.

Hauk was looking right at her now. His eyes asked the question. Would she stand by her own words of the other night?

Had she really meant what she'd told him?

If you dare to reach for me, I'll be reaching back....

Elli knew what to do then—and it had nothing to do with Kaarin's instructions. She stepped to the railing of the box. And she reached down her hand.

Hauk's strong fingers closed over hers.

"Yes," Elli said. "Yes, yes, yes, yes."

Chapter Seventeen

For a brief and shining moment, Elli reached down and Hauk reached up and there were only the two of them, hands clasped tight, her answer echoing between them.

But her father must have signaled for his men. They came running.

"Elli. Let go," her father commanded low and furiously.

The hell she would. She held on tight, and she scrambled to get over the too-high railing and into the strong arms that waited for her.

It was Hauk who stopped her. "No," he said. "He's right. Let go."

"No way." She held on tighter, craning down frantically toward him. "I told you. I'll never—"

He cut her off. "Let them take me. Stand firm. So will I."

"But I—" She got no chance to finish. The red-and-black coats were all around him. They dragged him back. She lost her hold.

He didn't struggle. He let them march him from the field.

The crowd had watched all this in total silence.

But as they saw the champion led away, the silence ended.

It started with a whisper that shivered through the stands. A whisper that built to a shout. The people rose from their seats and flooded the field. Someone threw a punch and someone hit back. And all of a sudden, there was a riot going on.

Elli couldn't tell whose side who was on. She couldn't tell if most of them were thrilled at what Hauk had done—or outraged.

Maybe, she decided, the people didn't know, either. The mock battle had laid the fire. And the sight of the champion being led off by the guard had struck the match. The blaze had gone instantly out of control.

Her father grabbed her arm. "This way. Now."

She supposed it would prove nothing to shake him off. She went where he took her, through an opening at the back of the box—along with Medwyn Greyfell, a couple of doddering old princes, Kaarin and two other ladies who'd been with them in the royal seats. They ran under the stands and came out on the grass about twenty yards from the trees. Her father's men materialized around them and led them on to safety.

* * *

They entered the palace through a service entrance similar to the one Elli had used the other night. The guards in the lead, they thundered up the narrow stairs and emerged into a wide hallway.

There, her father took charge. He sent the ladies and the elderly princes on their way. They fled eagerly, all too happy to escape a distinctly sticky situation. Within seconds, only Elli, her father, the Grand Counselor and the soldiers remained.

Her father turned a thunderous look on her. He spoke coldly to the guards. "Escort my daughter to her rooms. And see that she stays there."

Talk about medieval. What did he think? That she'd meekly allow them to lead her away? He should have asked Hauk about how well she took being held prisoner. The first guard dared to touch her sleeve.

"Get your hands off me."

The guard ignored her. He took one arm. A second guard moved in and took the other.

Before they could haul her off, Elli shouted, "Wait!" It worked. For a second, everyone froze. Elli spoke directly to her father. "Send them away. Give me a minute. Let me say what I have to say. Please."

The guards waited, still holding her.

At last, when she felt certain her father would bark out a curt order that would have the soldiers dragging her off, he raised a hand. "Release her."

The guards let her go.

"Leave us."

The guards—every one of them—tromped out through the door that led to the back stairs.

Finally, it was just Elli and her father and the Grand Counselor.

Elli didn't waste her chance. "Father, you're making a mistake," she said quietly. "There's no way you can make a prisoner of me—not if you imagine I'll ever speak willingly to you again. Not and have a prayer my mother might someday forgive you for whatever happened between you two all those years ago. This is the truth. I love Hauk. I want to marry him, and he's finally seen the light and admitted he wants to marry me. Give up whatever big plans you had for me. Let me go to the man that I love."

Her father's face now revealed nothing beyond a terrible composure that reminded her of Hauk. The wide hallway seemed to echo with her words—and with his tightly leashed fury.

She waited for him to shout for the guards again. But in the end, he only said softly, "Go to your rooms. Allow me a little time to…consider this situation."

She turned without another word and left him there.

"Admit it, old friend." Medwyn stood near the bust of Odin in Osrik's private audience room. "Your warrior has outfoxed us."

Osrik was still fuming. "My warrior. My *bastard* warrior."

"He is a fine man," said Medwyn, "bastard or not."

Osrik grunted. "Never in my wildest, most impossible imaginings would I have thought him a threat to our plan. Always, Hauk has known his place."

Medwyn chuckled. "That was before he met your daughter."

Osrik was pacing. He stopped and whirled on his friend. "You find this whole damnable mess amusing?"

"Wiser to laugh about it."

"My people are rioting."

"A good brawl, nothing more. It's probably over by now."

"There has to be a way to—"

"No."

"Medwyn, try to remember no one tells the king no."

"No one but his bloodbound, lifelong friend."

"And his own daughter." Osrik loosed a string of oaths.

When he fell silent, Medwyn said, "We are beaten, admit it. You saw the look that passed between them. *Inn makti murr.*" Medwyn said the words from the old language solemnly. "'The mighty passion.' No use in fighting *inn makti murr*. And Eric would never be a party to such a thing, anyway. We both know how he is. He'll never accept a wife who pines for another."

Osrik peered at his friend more closely. And then he stepped back. "I recognize that look. You knew. You knew all along."

Medwyn shrugged. "I suspected."

"Since when?"

"The night she came to this room to meet you for the first time. She expressed an excess of interest in your warrior, I thought."

"You said nothing." It was an accusation.

"I wasn't sure. And besides, I knew that if my suspicions were correct, we'd lost this gamble, anyway."

"Not necessarily. If you'd warned me before he declared himself so publicly, we might have—"

Medwyn waved his pale hand. "Doubtful. Fitz-Wyborn is almost as beloved by the people as your son was. As my son *is*. Were he to…disappear, there could be questions, investigations we'd never be able to control completely. And then there'd be your daughter to contend with. She's quite formidable. I doubt she'd simply accept that the man she loves has vanished."

"I was thinking a mission, a top-secret assignment…"

"Old friend, it's over. You know it. And you know you couldn't really do it, have FitzWyborn… eliminated. You're too fond of him."

"This is more important than my own petty emotions."

"Accept it. We've lost this battle. Declare Hauk high jarl, elevate him to legitimacy. Only the king can do it and you are the king. The Wyborns will love it. He does their name proud."

"I had hoped—"

"It is wiser, my dear friend, to put hope in a place where it will do you some good. Let Hauk go to the Wyborns, let him demand of them his marriage sword. Start planning a wedding fit for a treasured daughter." Medwyn laid a hand on Osrik's shoulder. "Consider it from this perspective. From what we know, the three sisters are very close. I doubt one of them would miss the wedding of another.''

Osrik shook his head. He could still see Elli, standing so proudly before him, demanding to be taken to the man that she loved. ''What a queen she would have made.''

''Be of good cheer,'' suggested Medwyn. ''You still have two other daughters. Both of them are unmarried. And nothing brings a woman running faster than a big wedding.''

Chapter Eighteen

In Gullandria, the wise couple marries on Friday as Friday is Frigg's day and Frigg is the goddess of hearth and home. As it happened, the summer solstice fell on a Friday that year. Osrik and Medwyn decided to combine a royal wedding and the annual celebration of Midsummer's Eve.

Thus, Elli married her Viking on June twenty-first, six weeks and four days after she'd first found him in her living room.

The vows themselves were exchanged in a broad, green field down in the palace parkland. A Lutheran minister presided over the vow-saying—after all, Gullandrians are good Christian folk.

Though tradition didn't call for attendants, Elli had two: her sisters. Brit and Liv had flown in from America for the event. Ingrid had ranted and railed at first, but then she'd finally realized that her daughter was in love. She'd ended up giving Elli her blessing and sending lavish gifts and her sincerest regrets that she wouldn't be at the wedding. Long ago she had vowed never again to set foot on Gullandrian soil.

Before the vow-saying, there was the presentation of swords, one provided by Osrik, one by the Wyborns to symbolize the traded power of the families. Then came the ceremony of the rings—exchanged, in true Viking style, on the ends of the marriage swords.

After the exchange of vows, the wedding party raced to the palace. Hauk, as tradition declared, arrived first. He barred the door with his marriage sword until his bride appeared and they could cross the threshold together.

In the great hall, the ceremonies continued: Hauk proved his strength by driving his sword into the heart of a tree trunk that had been cut and brought inside for the occasion; the new couple shared their first loving cup of ale. And Hauk set Mjollnir, Thor's hammer, in Elli's lap, a blessing said to ensure many strong, healthy children.

After the ceremonies, there was feasting and dancing and tale-telling by the best skalds in the land. Elli's sisters had a grand time. Many noted that both young women danced often with Finn Danelaw who seemed equally taken with each of the tall, proud American-raised princesses. It was remarked that young Prince Greyfell remained absent from the palace, though his father had contacted him and as good as commanded that he come to see his king's daughter wed.

Finally, well after midnight, the bride was led upstairs to the wedding chamber by her sisters and her ladies. Once she'd been properly prepared and lay beneath the covers in the wedding bed, the men—their way lit by torches—carried Hauk in. They stripped him of his wedding tunic and his fine, ruffled shirt and pulled off his boots and stockings, leaving his feet bare.

"Enough!" he boomed out once they got him down to only his black wedding breeches.

No one was going to argue with the king's warrior when he spoke so forcefully. They dragged him to the bed and pushed him down on it.

"Out," said Hauk. "Now." So at last, with much laughter and an excess of tasteless wedding-night advice, the men and the ladies left the bride and groom alone.

Hauk got up and locked the door behind them. He turned back to Elli, who looked like something straight out of the myths, her hair falling to her shoulders, her nightgown white as new snow.

"Wife," he said softly.

She threw back the covers and ran to him.

Their kiss was long and achingly sweet. When he raised his head, he said tenderly, "Tell me this is real and not just some dream I'm having."

She beamed up at him. "If it's a dream, we're both having it. If it's a dream, I ask only one thing."

"That we never wake up."

She laughed and nodded. "That's it. All I wish for."

He asked, "Are you sure you'll be happy as the wife of a soldier?"

She resisted the urge to roll her eyes. "Haven't we been through this about a hundred times?" She had decided to move to Gullandria. Hauk would finish out his commission. Already her father had offered her a number of positions, most of which included lots of glad-handing and photo-ops. She'd put Osrik off. She wanted a little time to get to know her new country without the added pressure of playing the princess— and to enjoy herself as a bride. "I am proud to be your wife," she said. "We'll figure it all out, day by day."

He still wore a too-serious expression. "I know you loved your work as a teacher."

She reached up and smoothed her fingers lightly over his furrowed brow. "Hauk. Stop it. I never make choices that I don't *want* to make. And anyway, I have a feeling I'll be teaching again someday."

"And your mother. I know you wanted your mother at your wedding."

"Yes, I did. But she didn't come. I'm not going to be sad about it. I'm only going to hope that someday she'll change her mind about returning here." She stood on tiptoe and pressed a kiss on his square chin. "This is no time for sadness, or for regrets. This…right now, is for you and for me."

A hot red light glowed from beyond the windows.

She grabbed his hand. "Come on. They've done it. They've set the ship on fire. Oh, come on, I have to see it."

She dragged him to the window. He stood behind

her, his strong arms around her, cradling her close to him, and they gazed down at the parkland behind the palace. Her father had ordered a proud Viking ship hauled into the open field where a month before Hauk had won the day and asked for his bride. The flames from the burning ship leaped high in the twilit sky. The long, graceful hull and the shape of the dragon's head at the prow could still be seen, gleaming golden, in the heart of the fire. Around it, people danced in joyous celebration.

"It's so beautiful," she whispered.

She felt his lips brush her hair.

And she couldn't wait a moment longer. She turned in his arms, slid her hands up that massive chest and clasped them around his neck. "Is it time, now, at last? Can we do...what married people do?"

His answer was a long, deep, soul-shattering kiss.

When he lifted his head, it was only to scoop her up high against his chest and to carry her back across the room to the bed.

He laid her down on it and he came down with her, fusing his mouth to hers, drinking her sweetness, stoking the fires between them to a white-hot blaze.

He kept kissing her, kept his mouth on her mouth, as he pulled away enough to get two handfuls of her gown. He gathered it in his fists and slid it up and up—until their kiss was broken.

But only for as long as it took him to drag the gown over her head and toss it to the rug beside the bed.

He claimed her mouth again, in hunger. In the need of a man for the woman he loves, the woman he has sworn to build a life with, the woman who will bear his children.

The children of a legal, consecrated union.

She fumbled at the lacings that tied his breeches, got them undone and off. And at last, they were both naked. Naked in their marriage bed, while the red-gold glow from the blazing ship and the soft glimmer of twilight bathed the room in burning light.

He kissed his way down her body, tasting a trail along the center of her, pausing to dip his tongue into her navel and then moving on....

Down...

She took his head in her hands as he pleasured her, as he did the things he did so well he had her writhing and begging and calling out his name.

And then, just at the moment when she knew she was finished, that she was on her way to fulfillment and there was no way to hold back, he slid up her body and seated himself within her in one clean, deep thrust.

Elli cried out.

The pleasure was so intense, the sensation so perfect, so exactly what she longed for. And he was there, with her. His face above her, his big body covering her, inside her—all hers.

She rolled her head on the pillow, drowning in a river of liquid fire, in a hot pool of purest erotic sensation.

"Elli." His voice was low, hoarse, dragged up from the depths of him. "Let me see your eyes."

She obeyed his command with a moan.

His eyes were waiting. He said, in a whisper of

passionate agony, "Elli. I love you. I love you. My wife..."

And then the rolling wonder began, up from the center of her, spreading out like a flame along every nerve ending, a fire in the heart of her, fire everywhere....

Her body closed around him, claiming him utterly. She called his name and he answered, "Elli."

And that was the best thing, the most beautiful thing of all.

That he could say her name now. Simply. With love.

At last, there was stillness.

Two cats—one black, one white—brought from California by Elli's sisters, cautiously emerged from beneath the bed where they'd scrambled to safety at all the shouting and laughing over the bedding of the bridal pair.

The cats jumped onto the bed, and sat together near the footboard. Diablo gave himself a bath. Doodles looked dreamy and purred with enthusiasm.

Hauk and Elli lay limp and satisfied, arms and legs entwined. Elli traced the thunderbolt and the tail of the dragon.

He whispered, "Forever."

She tipped her head back to look in his eyes again. "Oh, yes. Forever."

And then once more he kissed her, a kiss that started out so slow and sweet and then grew hotter, deeper, the banked fires licking higher, into flame.

Elli felt her heart rise up, into the endless twilight,

into the red glow from the ship that burned below them on the wide green field.

Born a princess, raised a happy, healthy American girl. But always wondering, always wishing, imagining what it might be like. If her mother hadn't left her father. If their family hadn't been torn apart.

Somehow, all that didn't matter quite as much anymore. She and Hauk were a family now. And *their* family would stay whole.

Love was what mattered. Love was what gave life order and dignity, beauty and meaning.

And for Elli Thorson Wyborn, love was right here.

In her warrior's arms.

* * * * *

If you enjoyed what you just read,
then we've got an offer you can't resist!

Take 2 bestselling love stories FREE!

Plus get a FREE surprise gift!

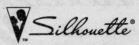

COMING NEXT MONTH

#1543 ONE IN A MILLION—Susan Mallery
Hometown Heartbreakers

FBI negotiator Nash Harmon was in town looking for long-lost family, not romance. But meeting Stephanie Wynne, the owner of the B & B where he was staying and a single mother of three, changed his plans. Neither could deny their desires, but would responsibilities to career and family keep them apart?

#1544 THE BABY SURPRISE—Victoria Pade
Baby Times Three

Wildlife photographer Devon Tarlington got the surprise of his life when Keely Gilhooley showed up on his doorstep with a baby. *His* baby. Or so she claimed. Keely was merely doing her job by locating the father of this abandoned infant. She hadn't expected Devon, or the simmering attraction between them....

#1545 THE ONE AND ONLY—Laurie Paige
Seven Devils

There was something mysterious about new to Lost Valley nurse-assistant Shelby Wheeling.... Dynamic doctor Beau Dalton was intrigued as much by her secrets as he was by the woman. Would their mutual desire encourage Shelby to open up, or keep Beau at arm's length?

#1546 HEARD IT THROUGH THE GRAPEVINE—Teresa Hill

A preacher's daughter was not supposed to be pregnant and alone. But that's exactly what Cathie Baldwin was...until Matthew Monroe, the onetime local bad boy, came along and offered the protection of his name and wealth. But who would protect *him* from falling in love...with Cathie *and* the baby?

#1547 ALASKAN NIGHTS—Judith Lyons

Being trapped in the Alaskan wilds with her charter client was not pilot Winnie Taylor's idea of a good time, no matter how handsome he was. Nor was it Rand Michaels's. For he had to remind himself that as a secret mercenary for Freedom Rings he was here to obtain information...not to fall in love.

#1548 A MOTHER'S SECRET—Pat Warren

Her nephew was in danger. And Sara Morgan had nowhere else to turn but to police detective Graham Kincaid. Now, following a trail left by the kidnapper, would Sara and Graham's journey lead them to the boy...and to each other?

SSECNM0503